The Escarpment

By

Bill Queen

For Tom Ward
very best wishes –
Bill Queen
05-07-02

Pittsburgh, PA

ISBN 1-56315-242-8

Paperback Fiction
© Copyright 2002 Bill Queen
All Rights Reserved
First Printing — 2001
Library of Congress #00-109359

Request for information should be addressed to:

SterlingHouse Publisher Inc.
The Sterling Building
440 Friday Road
Pittsburgh, PA 15209
www.sterlinghousepublisher.com

Cover Design: Jeffrey S. Butler — SterlingHouse Publisher, Inc.
Book Design: Kathleen M. Gall

Printed in Canada

The Escarpment

An original western novel based on fact.

*To Pansy ...
for making everything happen.*

Chapter 1

The saddle leather squeaked softly as he stepped down from his tall horse and tied up at the hitching rail. He loosened the girth, idly patting the animal's neck before negotiating the high step to the board walkway. He looked slowly up and down the street, squinting against the noon sun. The entire town was visible from where he was standing, fifteen or twenty buildings on each side of the only street. The sign overhead the door indicated food, drinks and rooms were available inside. He opened the door and walked into the shadowy interior.

He stood quietly just inside the swinging door for a few seconds, looking over the room with a practiced eye. The bartender and two other men were the only ones in the bar. As he looked at the bartender he was aware that he was also being looked over by the other three men. A hundred tiny important details registered in the stranger's mind, first and foremost that no man was wearing a gun. He had left his own six-gun and belt wrapped in his kit on the back of his horse, not wanting to appear armed as he entered the strange town.

His jeans and shirt were clean but well worn, his Stetson was Texas style, high crowned with a lanyard under his chin. He was fairly young, probably in his mid-thirties. Tall and slender, his skin was weathered and darkened by outdoor living. He stepped softly as he walked to the bar.

"Howdy," the stranger said as he put his foot comfortably on the bar rail. "Don't seem crowded today," this last with a smile.

"It just so happens that this is the noon rush," the bartender said as he grinned back. "What'll it be?"

"Cold beer if you got it."

"Comin' right up," the bartender said. "We get our ice from up in the mountains and haul it down every week or so. We're not so far from the snow line here." He set the big mug of beer on the bar.

The stranger took a long swallow and set the mug back on the bar. "Mighty good," he said. "It's been a while."

"Travelin' long?" the bartender asked.

"About three years," the stranger said, "all the way from Georgia."

"You must'a been in the war then?"

"Yep. I finished up my time in Andersonville."

"Is that so," the bartender said. "I hear'd that was a pretty bad place. You must'uv been one a' the lucky ones."

"Yeah, I guess you could say that," the stranger said. "I was only there a few weeks before the war ended." But a few weeks in hell is enough to last a lifetime, he thought.

"We got a man who lives up at the edge of the mountains that was at Andersonville," the bartender said.

"Is that a fact. His name wouldn't be Roll Jacobs by any chance, would it?" the stranger asked.

"Matter of fact, it is. You wouldn't happen to know him would you?" the bartender asked rhetorically.

"Yeah, I would. He told me to look him up if I ever got out this way and that's what I'm gonna' do."

The bartender rocked back on his heels and studied the stranger intently.

"Maybe I better explain a little bit," the stranger said. "Roll and I are old friends and he invited me to stop at his place if I was ever out this way. That was back in eighteen and sixty-five. My name's London and I'm sure Roll will make me welcome. Just so you'll know I ain't up to no mischief."

"Maybe so," the bartender said. "It's just that Roll don't have a lot of truck with strangers showing up at his place. I never knowed of any visitors showing up unannounced before."

"When we got released from Andersonville," London answered, "he told me that if I ever got to Denver, just head north along the

Rockies and sooner or later I'd find someone who would know where he was at. Sounds like you might just be that someone."

"Hey stranger!" came a shout from across the room. "I'm the man you're lookin' for. I can tell you how to get to Jacob's spread."

London stepped away from the bar and walked towards the old man who was doing the talking. He was a desert rat type, well worn and dirty looking. His bushy whiskers had obviously not had any attention in months and tobacco stains ran all the way from his mouth to his belt buckle. His quick, high-pitched voice was equally irritating.

"Hell's fire," he went on, "if you're gonna' cause trouble for Jacobs, I might even lead you to his place. I ain't had no use for him ever since he run me off from prospectin' along the Escarpment."

"No, I ain't gonna' cause him no trouble, he's an old friend and I just want'a go see him," London replied.

"Well, either way," the old man said, "his place ain't that hard to find. Just ride north for two days and you'll come to a pass between them two big peaks you see up there with the snow on them." He pointed out the front windows towards the mountains visible in the distance.

"At about the tree line, a valley cuts down and there's only one way to go. If you keep riding another half a day you'll come to the edge of the Escarpment and that's where you'll find him and his clan. The way ain't hard to follow with all the broke down wagons and junk along the trail."

"What's this Escarpment you mentioned," London asked.

"Oh, you'll see when you get there," the old man said. "Some people who seen it claim it could be the end of the world. For sure you won't see any Injuns up there. They claim the place is haunted and full of evil spirits an' I ain't so sure they're wrong."

"Okay, grandpa, an' thanks for the directions," London said as he returned to the bar.

"The old man told you right," the bartender said. "He's just mad cause Roll won't let him prospect in the hills around where he lives. Don't rightly know why, but Roll just likes to keep to himself, 'cept for his family, that is."

"How big a family has Roll got?" London asked.

"I ain't sure a' that either," the bartender answered. "I know he's got a dozen kids, more or less, and a bunch of his wife's people live up there. Roll himself comes to town two or three times a year to pick up supplies and such. They come in wagons and there are other men with him. I always just supposed that the men were his wife's kinfolk. They never have much to say, they just pick up their goods and leave. Never even known them to stay overnight."

"So about how far is it up to Roll's place?" London asked.

"Oh, it'd be near to two days on horseback. I'd guess at least three or four days by wagon, even if you hurried along," the bartender said.

London drained the last of his schooner and asked for another. Then he said, "I see by your sign you got rooms to rent. I think I'll just stay here tonight and sleep somewhere besides on the ground. Tomorrow morning will be early enough to start, seein' as it's taken me this long to get this far."

"Yep, we got rooms. Will you be wantin' vittles? They're fifty cents extra and the room's two bits and beer is a nickel a mug."

London fished around in his shirt pocket and dropped a one-dollar gold piece on the bar. "Give me another cold beer and before the evening's over I figure to drink up the change."

The bartender set the frosty mug on the bar and London picked it up and retreated to one of the empty tables along the wall. He sat and leaned back, his spurless boots resting on the tabletop as he enjoyed the luxury of furniture and a roof over his head.

I've come a long way from Gettysburg and the war in the last three years, he thought. Yeah, three years and two thousand miles and I can still smell the camp and the death that was penned up there. I wonder if it bothers Roll as much as it still bothers me?

Three hours later London came down the steps from his room and smiled sheepishly at the bartender. "Your beds are extra soft. All I did was carry my gear upstairs and sit down on the bed. Now it's three hours later."

London had been awakened when the bartender had yelled up the steps that his dinner was ready and had responded to a meal of steak and beans. The food was acceptable only so far as he hadn't had to cook it him self and any changes were welcome after so long on the trail. His gear was in the first room at the top of the stairs and his horse was settled into a warm and dry stable just down the street.

Across the room, the bartender and his wife, a cowboy referred to simply as 'Tex' and the two old men were involved in a raucous poker game for match sticks. London caught the attention of the bartender and waved his empty beer mug.

"Help yourself," was the response. "You still got two to go on your money."

London drew his beer from the spigot and wandered over to the table where the card game was in progress.

"Want'a join in?" the bartender's wife asked. "Everyone gets a hundred match sticks to start and when they loose'em they're done until one person wins all the matches and then we start all over again."

"Sure, don't mind if I do," London said spinning a chair around and sitting down between the two old men. It was just dark outside and the coal oil lamps cast a warm and comfortable glow over the room.

The game went along at a lively pace as the bartender's wife slowly accumulated a pile of matches. The old prospector was the first one eliminated when he pushed his luck and bet three queens and ran into a small straight in the cowboy's hand. He turned his chair around as was customary for the vanquished and rested his arms along the back.

"Stranger," the prospector said, "there was somethin' I seen when I was up near Jacob's spread that has always bothered me. Maybe if you go there, you can check it for me?"

"What's that?" London asked looking up from his cards.

"I didn't see no outhouses. There was a bunch of small houses and a goodly bunch of people but I never seen a single shithouse. Now you tell me, how could that many people live without havin' to go to the toilet."

"Bet two," the cowboy said. "You just must'a not looked good, old man. There had'da been some around somewhere."

The game went on as the prospector said, "An' something else. Old Roll himself met me at the edge of the houses and made it clear that I had to leave before dark. They wouldn't even let me go in one of the houses for a bite to eat, they just made me a couple of sandwiches and had me eat them standing at the edge of the corral. That an' a cup of coffee was all I got."

It occurred to London that this man's whining voice and attitude could soon get on his nerves. He drew two cards and kept his mouth shut.

"Dealer takes one," the woman said and she looked over at the prospector and continued. "Maybe you had just been in the hills too long and was getting' a bit gamey, if you catch my drift."

They all laughed, even the prospector and he responded by saying, "No way is that so. I always wash up and put on a clean shirt before going visitin'. I just got a funny feelin' about that place up there."

"I check," the cowboy said looking towards London.

London stared at the cards in his hand, his mind wandering back to the days on the Mississippi riverboats, first as just a gambler and later working security for the owners. His main job had been to keep tinhorns and cheaters from fleecing the passengers who enjoyed the luxury of the floating palaces at the end of the war.

Many things in his life had gone to make him the man he was, not the least of which was his upbringing by his uncle, a Minnesota marshal who had taught him the six-gun at an early age. London knew he had a natural ability with weapons. Good eyes, strength, nerves and snake like reflexes all went to make him the best anyone had ever seen. He practiced-every day for years and years under his uncle's supervision. Only the war had taken him away from his uncle's influence. And then Antietam and Andersonville had changed …

"I check," the cowboy said slightly louder.

"Oh … sorry," London said, "I drop," and he tossed his cards onto the table.

The cowboy, who had never heard the prospector's story before said, "Why did they tell you to be gone before dark?"

"I never been able to figure that out," the old man replied. "Just that I was to be gone beyond the tree line before the sun went down. An' when I left, I knowed someone was followin' to make sure I did just that."

"Maybe you was imagining," the cowboy said as he picked up his cards and started sorting them.

"Ain't no way I imagined it! I been around Injuns all my born days and I know when someone's snoopin' around. An' one more thing. When I was ridin' out of the valley, I heard this sound like a horse that had been run too far and too long, only a hundred times as loud. The onlyest place it could'a come from was Roll Jacobs spread an' I been puzzlin' about that sound more than anything ever since."

The poker game had slowed to a stop and London leaned back and studied the old man with more interest. He didn't know how much to believe but his feeling had become more negative towards the story-teller. London could think of a dozen or more reasons to run this man off if he came nosing around.

The game went on but the mood had changed. The night seemed darker and the shadows deeper as the specter of mystery had invaded all of their thoughts.

Chapter 2

London came down the steps early and found the bartender's wife at work in the kitchen. He settled at a table after getting a cup of coffee in the kitchen and being assured his breakfast was on the way. Thirty minutes later with bacon, beans, bread and biscuits under his belt, he walked the hundred feet or so to the general store to replenish his supplies.

"Mornin'," the storekeeper said. "You must be the stranger who rode in on the tall horse yesterday. What can I do for ya'?"

"Mornin'," London responded. "I need to pick up a few things like coffee, beans, side of bacon, salt and sugar. An' I need a new coffee pot and a couple boxes of those new .22 shells if you got any."

"Yessir, I do. We got a case in about six months ago but I ain't sold many. We only got four rifles in stock that shoot them shells and around here the only thing they're good for is rattlers and prairie chickens and such. Most everyone still carries the .44's when they go inta' the mountains. Rifles and pistols both shootin' the same ammunition is pretty handy."

As the shopkeeper talked he was scurrying around the store filling London's order. "Where you headed for, stranger, if you don't mind me askin'?"

"Goin' up to see an old friend of mine who's got a spread somewhere north of here name a' Roll Jacobs. You know him?"

"Surely do," the storekeeper said. "I do a lot'a business with Roll. Matter of fact I'm holding an order for him in the back room now. If you see him, just tell him it's here."

"Maybe I could save him a trip and take it up to him," London offered.

"Taint likely, stranger, lessen you can pack a dozen big anvils an' eighteen double blade plows in your saddle bags. It's more or less Roll's usual order about every three months."

"What's a man want with a dozen anvils?" London asked.

"Beats me," the storekeeper said. "It's just that Roll has a standing order for the plows and the anvils every time I get in a load of supplies. He gets a bunch of other stuff along with 'em, but he always gets those things for sure. Him and his kin bring at least half a dozen wagons to town every time they get supplies. Sometimes when they got a special big order, it looks like a damn parade comin' and goin'."

"Huh," London exclaimed, "maybe he's tradin' with the Indians or somethin'. He must have some reason for getting the stuff."

"Well it might be the Indians. Around here we got the Nez Perce. You know anything about them stranger?"

"Only that I heard they ain't hostile and pretty much stay to them-selves."

"Well, that's mostly true," the storekeeper said, "but it goes a little further than that."

"You got time to tell me about it?" London asked.

The storekeeper looked around at the room full of merchandise with just the two of them standing at the counter and laughed. "Mister, I can stand here an' talk all day and not miss a lick a' business."

The storekeeper pulled a high stool up to the counter and sat, resting his forearms on the wood in front of him. Then he reached out his hand and said, "By the way, my name's Len Stork."

London shook the offered hand and said, "Folks call me London."

"Now about the Nez Perce, a little bit tells a lot about them. It seems to everyone around here that they're the boss Injuns in this part of the country. Shoshone, Sioux, Comanche all take a wide walk around the Nez Perce. They're probably the smartest and quietest Indians around but when there's trouble, they're the damnedest fighters that was ever born. And they got these horses called Appaloosas. I don't know if you ever seen one but they're kinda' gray with dark spots on their rear legs and hindquarters. Them what's had experience with 'em claim they're the best horse ever."

"Is'zat so," London said, having reservations in his own mind about the horse information.

"Yep, an' the only ones I ever seen, other than the ones the Indians was ridin' was the two that Roll and his son rode to town one day with the wagons. Always figured he traded with the Indians and that made me even more sure."

"Anyway," the storekeeper went on, "chances are if you run into any Indians around here it's gonna' be the Nez Perce so if you just mind your manners and keep moving, you ain't gonna' have any trouble."

"Len, you been a big help," London said pulling coins from his shirt pocket and paying the amount that the storekeeper had figured up on a scrap of wrapping paper. "And I'll be sure and tell Roll you got his goods if I see him."

"Friend, if you keep riding north from here, you're gonna' see him or fall off the end of the world. Good day to you."

"So long to you," London said as he pulled the door shut behind him and headed for the livery stable, the information rattling around in his head like a dozen anvils.

When London arrived at the stables he found his horse freshly brushed and combed by the son of the owner and he gave the boy a nickel for his work.

"Gee, thanks, Mister," the boy had said, "but I just like animals and this is shore a mighty fine horse."

The boy had even beaten his saddle blanket on a rail until it was good and soft.

London looked to his right and saw that the sun was already half way to noon as he rode out of town. The abundance of fleecy clouds made him think that he was going to see rain about tonight or tomorrow so he planned to camp on high ground where there would be a tree to hang his canvas.

He could make out the faint tracks of wagons following the natural terrain of the land and he let his horse canter along at it's own pace.

London looked ahead at the mountains and the two biggest snow covered peaks didn't look that far away, but he had learned long ago the distances in the clear air were very deceptive. The town people said he wouldn't reach the valley between the peaks until tomorrow. When he did, he would be above the tree line and then he would start riding downhill until he came to the Escarpment and Roll's ranch. Since leaving town he had been gradually going up but the slope was gentle and his horse was handling it easily.

About mid afternoon he rested and made coffee in his new pot and ate half a loaf of bread he had saved from his breakfast. He hobbled his horse and let him graze near a small stream. After about an hour he got moving again and pushed on until dark. Aside from the magnificent country, the only moving creatures he had seen that day were a few elk and in the distance an abundance of antelope that had watched him curiously and barely moved out of his way. Only the faint tracks of passing wagons indicated any human presence.

About dark he saw a stand of big ponderosa pines a couple of hundred yards off the trail on a small hillock. Protection from the weather and a stream nearby were all the inducements London needed to call it a day and fix his coffee, beans and bacon. He hung his sheet of canvas over a tree limb and staked it down in case of rain and by full dark, he let his fire go out. He puzzled for a short time over what he might find when he reached his destination and was soon sound asleep, a man at ease with the world around him.

He woke at daylight, had coffee, beans and the last of his bread and a half hour later was on the trail with the tree line now in sight just a few hours away. The rise was steeper now and the valley narrower. Then he saw the Indians.

There were six of them on their horses about fifty yards back from the wagon trail and as he approached he saw that there were four grown men and two boys about ten years old. They were all dressed in buckskin and carried short bows over their shoulders. Quivers of arrows hung from a rawhide strap fastened around their waists. Their horses were the Appaloosas, exactly what he had been told to expect.

There were no saddles or bridles of any kind; the riders just sat on their horses as naturally as a white man would sit on a kitchen chair. As he approached, they all stood still, the horses scarcely moving as they watched him come towards them.

London was still in the roadway and about to pass the point closest to the Indians when he looked directly at them and held both of his hands out, shoulder high with his palms facing away from him.

"Morning, gentlemen," London said, hoping he was doing the right thing.

To his extreme surprise one of the Indian boys answered with a nod and said, "Good morning to you," in perfect English.

The six riders turned and began riding off as one. London had seen no movement or signs between man and beast, just suddenly they all moved at the exact same time and began cantering towards a distant hilltop. London was more than slightly impressed at the horsemanship he had just witnessed. They never once looked back but London sat still and watched them until they disappeared from sight.

Very interesting when a bunch of wild Indians meet you on the trail and wish you well in your own language. A strange country for sure. Yes sir, I surely do wonder what will happen next.

It was a little after noon when he broke over a rise and saw a valley spreading before him. It was maybe two more hours down to the tree line and it seemed the valley narrowed down there. He had been told it widened out to a grassy meadow after a few miles and from below the trees you could see all the way to Jacob's spread.

He had been watching his back trail ever since he had seen the Indians but they had completely disappeared after riding over a hilltop and he had pretty much put them out of his mind. Now he was just hoping to make the ranch by dark. He had taken a half-hour break about noon but since they were now going downhill, the traveling was a lot easier.

When London broke through the tree line and saw the valley stretching he could only stop and stare. It had to be one of the most beautiful sights he had ever seen in all his days in the west. Far away, in the clear air, he could make out a cluster of houses and in between was at least ten miles of blue-green grass that moved in the wind like a giant pool of water. This is what heaven must look like if I ever get to see it, he thought.

"Howdy, partner. What can I do for you?"

Chapter 3

London spun in his saddle to see a figure sitting on a horse with the sun at his back. The horse was identical to the ones he had seen the Indians riding earlier but the man, as near as he could make out with the sun in his eyes, was a white man.

"Howdy," London said, squinting his eyes and moving his horse gently to the side to get a better look.

The man was young, about twenty; heavy in the shoulders and stocky built. He was dressed more like a farmer than a cowboy; plaid shirt, jeans, Stetson, boots, but no chaps or jacket or work saddle on the horse. One thing he did have was one of the new Henry repeating rifles resting across the saddle in front of him, it's muzzle pointed negligently at the ground between them.

"I'm lookin' for a man and this is supposed to be his spread. Can you tell me if this is the Jacob's ranch?"

"Yeah, it is. An' what you be wantin' to see Roll Jacobs for?" the man asked, neither friendly or hostile but very business like.

London was impressed by the mature manner of the young man and, as he got a clearer look, he could begin to see the resemblance to the man who was probably his father. Wide apart brown eyes, direct gaze, square chin, thick muscular body were all indicative of what London remembered about Roll.

"He's an old friend and he told me if I ever got to this part of the country to look him up."

"An what be your name, stranger?" the young man asked.

"London."

"London what? That your first name or your last name?"

"Just London," London answered. "That's my name."

The man broke into a smile that was one of the friendliest London had ever seen, another indicator of who his father might be.

"Mr. London," the young man said, "I often heard my Pa speak of you an' he always said if you was ever to show up here at the front door, you was to be brought right straight on to the houses. My name's Joshua but everyone jus' calls me Josh. I surely am pleased to make your acquaintance," and he guided his horse close just using his feet and stuck out his hand.

"My pleasure, Josh," London said shaking the rough and powerful hand of the boy about half his age.

The boy stepped down off his horse and slid the rifle into a scabbard attached to his saddle. Then he fished a mirror from his saddlebags and began flashing it towards the houses. "Got'ta let them know we're comin," he explained.

In less than a minute, an answering flash could be seen from the houses and Josh mounted up and began to lead the way down the hillside.

"What was the signal for?" London asked.

"Oh, just somethin' Pa wants us to do," Josh said casually.

Too causally, London thought.

London watched the boy ride, his reins hanging in a knot on the front of his saddle. Never once did he use them to guide his horse, just rode with his hands resting in front of him as he talked with London, much as the Indians had ridden.

"How far is it to the ranch house?" London asked squinting in the afternoon sun.

"'Bout two hours at the rate we're goin' now," Josh answered. "Ain't no sense in hurryin' since we're gonna' be there in plenty of time for supper anyway."

"How'd you come to be riding out this way?" London asked. "Hunting or something?"

"Naw, it was just my two days in the trees," Josh said. "Pa has us come out and take turns watchin' for strangers and bein' kind of a welcoming committee. Our job is to make sure everyone comes straight to the house and not go wandering around causing mischief or whatever."

"You mean there's always someone up here keepin' watch for anyone coming in?" London asked.

"Yep, but just for strangers. Folks we know or the Indians don't need a guide."

"Will things be all right while you're gone from up there bringing me in?" London asked

"Sure. That was another reason I gotta' signal before startin' in. Right now another rider is on the way here from the ranch to keep watch since I had'a leave the trees."

Even as Josh spoke, London could see in the distance a rider coming towards them, pushing his horse at a good gallop. As the rider neared, it was apparent that the horse was another of the Appaloosas, its powerful hindquarters pumping as it held the fast pace with little effort.

"Hey, Josh," the rider yelled as he approached, "what's going on an' who's the stranger?"

"Hey, Zack," Josh answered, reining in his horse. "This's London, the man Pa talked about and said might be comin'. I'm takin' him in so you'll have to keep watch 'til someone comes to relieve you."

"We thought there might be trouble when we seen your signal," Zack said. He turned to London and held out his hand and it was obvious that Zack was a slightly younger version of Josh Jacobs.

"I'll be seein' you in camp in a day or so, Mr. London. Now I gotta' go." With no sign of guidance that London could discern, Zack's horse again set out at a gallop, headed back the way they had just come, his duties obviously very much on his mind.

As they rode on, London saw the valley spreading out to the sides, wider and wider, something that could not be seen from where he had entered. Ahead, as the settlement came more into focus, the mountains far in the distance did not change at all and were snow-covered, mottled with sunshine and shade and breathtakingly beautiful.

"I can't help but notice that you and your brother were both riding the same kind of horse," London said. "Do you raise them here?"

"Yeah, we do now. Pa got them by trading with Chief Ouseph way back when," Josh answered.

"Who's Chief Ouseph?" London asked.

"He's the big chief of the Nez Perce. Him and Pa are friends and he comes to visit every once in a while." Josh said.

London pondered that for a minute and then said, "The Indians are friendly then?"

"Yep, we get along with 'em real good. You'll be seein' some Indian young'uns when we get to the ranch."

"How come you got young Indians at your ranch?" London asked.

"Oh, Pa'll have to explain that," Josh said

London was not getting a lot of answers to his questions and it was bothering him a bit. He believed Josh could have enlightened him but had, for some reason, chosen not to do so. He guessed that he and Roll would have a lot to talk about.

Chapter 4

There was much to see and digest for London as he rode into the ranch. More than a dozen houses were set in a semi-circle and all seemed to face away from him. About a mile off to the right were several other buildings that looked like barns and workshops, maybe a smith's shop, London thought. There was smoke coming from the chimneys of a couple of the buildings.

The houses seemed to have been built around a central park with trees and flowers that were well manicured and showed considerable care. In the center was a tall flag pole and a large flag of solid red color waved from its top.

People were scattered about, all standing quietly and watching him ride in, interested but contained. As he got close enough, he saw that the man standing nearest the flagpole was Roll Jacobs. Next to him was a handsome woman of middle age, tall and full figured with mixed gray and brown hair giving the best indication of her age. London saw Roll's face light up as he recognized him and stepped forward purposely for a greeting. London dropped from his horse and stepped forward just in time to be engulfed in a huge bear hug and Roll exclaimed for all to hear, "Praise be, it's London. Let me look at you, old friend," and he gripped London by the shoulders with his big, powerful hands and stared into his face.

"Of all the people I have ever known, you're the one I would most want to see ride in," Roll said.

London knew he had reached the end of a long journey as he said. "I'm mighty glad to see you too, old friend."

Roll turned to the woman near the flagpole and yelled out, "Come here, Helen. This is the man I've told you so much about."

London watched as Helen walked towards them, taller that average with an athletic appearance and a weathered look that indicated a welcome relationship with the outdoors.

Her handshake was firm but then she gathered London in a close hug and said, "My husband has told me something of you. Thank you so much for saving his life and all you did for him during the war." She had tears in her eyes as she stretched her neck and kissed him on the cheek.

London was slightly embarrassed by the show of affection and mumbled something about his duty and so on but words really failed him at such an emotional welcome.

"Thank you, ma'am. It's my pleasure," he finally stammered.

"Come and sit," Roll said, leading London to a picnic table near the flagpole. "I'm sure you gotta' be hot, dry and hungry. The women will bring some refreshments here in the shade. We got so much to talk about, I don't know where to begin."

London sat down in a wicker chair and looked around. There was so much to take in that he didn't know where to begin with questions about the ranch and all of his surroundings.

Just as London decided to ask about the flag, Josh called out, "Hey, Mr. London. I'll take your horse to the barn and put him up for you. Don't worry none, I know about horses."

London waved at Josh and turned to Roll, saying, "I can see he does know horses. Mighty nice young fella you got there."

"Yeah, we been lucky with our kids," Roll answered. "We got eight of them, five girls and three boys."

"That's great," London said. "I never had much family and I always envied those that had lots of kin. Now tell me about your place here. For instance, what's the red flag for?"

Roll looked up shrugged. "Just a decoration," he said. "We change it every once in a while. Here at the Escarpment we do things a little different than most folks."

"I've heard that word several time in the last few days. Just why is this place called the Escarpment ranch?" London asked. "Looking at all those mountains in the distance there," and he nodded away from the houses and towards the northwest, "I'd of thought the mountains would have been a better name."

Roll paused while he considered London's question and the hesitation caught London's attention. It seemed to him that every time he asked a question, there were pauses and thoughtful consideration before it was either partly answered or avoided altogether.

I'm gonna' have to start paying more attention, London thought. I can't really believe everything is not entirely on the up and up with Roll Jacobs being involved, but all I really know about him is what he told me at Andersonville. Everyone has things they don't want to talk about. London's mind snapped back to just after Roll had come under his care and someone had mentioned the battle of Antietam and Roll had just collapsed and sat with his head in his hands, crying softly for several hours until he finally brought his emotions back under control. London thought he understood but it was something they had only mentioned to each other one time after that.

"About this being called the Escarpment," Roll went on, "if you'll just bear with Helen and me for a couple hours, we'll show you why the place has that name. Believe us, it will be worth the wait."

As Roll spoke, Helen reached over and took his hand, nodded to her husband and smiled at London.

"Now," Roll said, "tell us what you been doing for the last three years."

"There's not all that much to tell," London said. "After we split up in Memphis, I headed south to New Orleans to relax and rest up from the war and prison. I had the money you gave me and it was more than enough to let me get my life back together. By the way, I still got that money in my saddle bags and I'll give it back the next time you and my horse are near each other."

"You don't have to do that," Roll said. "It was a token of appreciation for what you did for me in the prison."

London looked straight at Roll and said, "If you was me, would you want to pay back the man that let you get your life going again? I ain't saying I didn't use the money to get my feet back on the ground, 'cause I did. But I had a run of pretty good luck since the war and I got you to thank for it. Anyway, you're getting the money back and that's the end of that."

London said this last with a smile but it was clear that he WOULD give Roll the money.

"Okay, okay, let's forget that for now," Roll said. "Tell us what else you been up too."

"Maybe I better start back a ways since I don't know how much you told Helen about me," London said.

"My folks was killed when I was young," London started, "and I was sent to live with an uncle up in the plains of Minnesota. He was a town marshal and he raised me as best he could. He saw I got my schooling and that I learned to do my chores. And he taught me one other important thing—how and when to use a gun."

"By the time I was about seventeen, I was about full grown and he started using me for one of his deputies. Before the war we had trouble with Indians as much as the whites and he taught me to treat everyone alike, hard but fair. My uncle considered any disregard of the law should be punished and he made sure I followed his example."

"But I had this knack for the six-gun; muzzle loader, cap and ball, Colt, anything that would shoot. I was straight and the fastest anyone had ever seen. When the war came it put me in good stead with the army and more than once made the difference between living and dying. But it still didn't keep me out of Andersonville."

"This is where Roll and I met for the first time. I remember the morning they brought him inside the front gate and left him laying there on the ground. One of the odd things was that one of the men they brought in with him and left on a stretcher was dead and had been dead for a while. Why they even took the time to carry him inside was beyond me."

As London talked he never looked at Roll or Helen, just stared off at the mountains with a faraway detached look in his eyes. "Roll had been shot through and through in his right hip and his left shoulder was dislocated. He was bad, but it looked to me like with a little care he would pull through."

"Me and three of my unit were together," London went on, "and the first thing we had to do was fix Roll's shoulder. We pulled the arm out and got the bones back into alignment. After that all we could do was keep the bullet wound clean and hope for the best. There were no doctors or medicine anywhere in the camp and we learned early on that if you sent a man outside for treatment, he never came back."

"But Roll was tough," London continued, "and within a week he was walking by himself. From there on we just managed to get by and suddenly one day the guards came and opened the gates and told us the war was over. The prisoners began to stumble out of the camp and it was three days before we found out the Rebs had lost the war."

"Roll and I hooked up with a Union patrol headed for Memphis and they let us ride in a wagon and gave us food. After we got to Memphis, I found out Roll had been an officer and was a rich man. He went to the telegraph office and sent off a message. Three days later a bank gave him a pile of money. Roll left on a river boat headed north to hook up with the railroad and get back to Washington to settle with the army and I went south with the stake he gave me. I did promise to come here to the ranch when we parted company."

"I started out as a gambler on the riverboats and ended up being a trouble shooter protecting the passengers from the riffraff."

"What do you mean?" Helen asked.

"Like I said before," London answered, "I was always good with a gun and after a few incidents on different boats I got kind of a reputation. Anyway different owners of riverboats came and asked me to keep the tinhorns and cheaters under control. I guess I had the right qualifications being a gambler and a gunfighter of sorts. It paid damn—oops—sorry, darn good and with what I could win at the tables I was soon pretty well fixed."

"How long did you do this?" Roll asked.

"A couple years," London said. "Then some cattle men asked me to be a buyer for them out in Texas and arrange to get the cattle to the railroads. It was rough country and even rougher men to deal with but I managed for about another year and then one day I was just tired of it all. I packed my traveling gear behind my saddle and headed west."

"How long did it take you to get here?" Roll asked.

"I left Dallas early April and I guess about eight or nine weeks on the trail. I didn't hurry none, just kept moving and knew I'd get here sooner or later," London said.

"You make it all sound routine," Helen said. "I'm sure it must have been a pretty exciting time."

"After the war, nothing was unusual," London answered. "Winding down from the violence and learning to live with normal people again was the hardest part."

"What was the hardest part?" a woman's voice from behind him asked.

London turned and looked up at a tall young woman standing behind him. She was holding a large serving tray covered with plates, food, glasses, pitcher of lemonade and a stack of silverware. But it was not the tray that seized London's attention.

Her clear, wide apart brown eyes were the first things he saw. After that, everything else about the woman imprinted itself on his mind. Reddish-brown hair, athletic figure and classical features were all part of what he believed was the most beautiful woman he had ever seen. He pulled his mouth closed so he wouldn't appear to be a complete fool although he continued to stare.

"What was the hardest part?" she asked the second time.

"Getting used to beautiful people after the war," London replied, recovering from the start the woman had caused with his self-possession.

"This is our oldest daughter, Colleen," Roll said. "She takes a little getting used to."

"At least you could tell me who's getting all this food I carried out here," she said.

Helen spoke up making the introduction. "This is London, the man who saved your father's life at Andersonville. He's just been telling us what has been keeping him busy these last few years."

"How do you do," Colleen said very formally as she offered her hand to be shaken.

As he took her hand, London was still unsettled by the eyes of the woman.

"And is your name London something or something London," she asked.

"Ahhhh—my name is—ah—just London. That's all the name I ever needed."

He watched her smile of amusement at his discomfort and inwardly resolved himself back under control. He knew he was appearing to be something of a bumpkin in her eyes.

"Well, if you were talking about Andersonville, I'm glad I missed the conversation. From what father has said, that place had to be an abomination on earth."

"That it was," London admitted, "but that place is also a fact of life. It happened."

"It just goes against everything I believe in," Colleen said. "Man's inhumanity should never be allowed to go to those limits."

"Colleen, set that food down and pour the drinks while I explain to London," Roll said. "You see, Colleen is a doctor and she takes suffering in a very personal way."

"A woman doctor!" London said incredulously. "A real medical doctor!?"

Colleen handed London a glass of lemonade and said, "So you're one of those."

"One of what?" London asked.

"I guess that's what we're going to have to wait and see," Colleen answered as she set down with a solid thump next to her mother.

London looked down at the tray of food that Colleen had placed before him and watched as Helen poured lemonade for everyone. The tray held a plate with fried potatoes, six chicken legs and a fourth of an apple pie.

"Why don't I eat this snack," London said, "while you tell me about your place here?"

Roll Jacobs took a deep breath and looked at his wife. "This is something I don't very often get a chance to do," he said. "I'm going to tell you my story up until the end of the war."

"My father and Helen's father were partners in business back in the east. They were both engineers and they worked on building the canal systems in the early days of the 1800's. They invested heavily in the Erie Canal and made a lot of money. Then they helped build a railroad between the Great Lakes and the East Coast and made even more money."

Roll put his arm around his wife's shoulders as he went on. "Helen was an only child but I had three brothers, all older. Our parents believed in education and Helen went to school to be a teacher, but after a couple of years, against her parent's wishes she switched to engineering and graduated first in her class. It was almost unheard of at the time for a woman to be in such a profession and to work with her brain as well as her hands."

"For me," Roll said, "I had three brothers and they had all been educated in Europe, one a doctor, one a lawyer and the third became an engineer like our father. I was the youngest and maybe the wildest, so I talked my father into getting me an appointment at West Point."

"I did well at the Point and graduated in '41," Roll went on, "just in time for the Mexican War and I was subsequently appointed to the staff of General Jefferson Davis as a Second Lieutenant. At the time I was excited about the prospect of war and making a name for myself in the military service."

"For nearly two years we fought along the Rio Grande, sometimes on one side of the border and sometimes on the other side. It was a grim business and I saw enormous suffering by both the military and the civilians, who were victimized unmercifully. I learned in short order that war was not a noble undertaking. Cruel, vicious and sadistic men heaped atrocities on their supposed enemies."

London finished the last of his chicken and started on his pie, all the time listening with rapt attention as Roll spoke.

"By '43," Roll continued, "things had pretty much been resolved and I couldn't take no more. I resigned my commission and returned to Pennsylvania where Helen and I were married six months later. We had decided to head west and set up our home in the new land that was opening up in the northwest."

As Roll talked his wife had taken his hand in hers and Colleen had leaned her head against her father's shoulder. They both knew how painful were the memories of the Mexican Campaign.

"Helen and I started west in the spring of '45 and were gearing up in St. Louis when we got word from the east that both our parents had been killed in an explosion and fire aboard a riverboat near Louisville. There was nothing we could do so we had my brothers handle the arrangements and we headed for the northwest on an early wagon train, one of the first to attempt the crossing."

"It was a fairly simple trek," Roll continued. "The Indians paid us little notice and we were part of a huge train, over a hundred wagons. We had four wagons of our own and enough servants to make the crossing without much discomfort."

Roll stood up from the table, took a long drink of lemonade and stretched his arms and back. "From here on we're all in the story," he said.

"It was when we skirted the badlands and started into the mountains that the only real problem developed. You see, few trains had crossed through the area and as we searched for a pass, we were continually turned back by the rough terrain. After several aborted attempts to make our way through, we were again turned back and then we came to this place. When the train turned back and continued to search, Helen and I saw the potential of the valley for a home. Good grass, trees of all types for lumber, protection from the elements by the surrounding mountains and the peace and solitude we had been seeking. And also, the Escarpment."

Roll stood and both women rose with him, anticipating what was coming next.

"Over this way," Roll said to London, "there's something we all want you to see."

The four of them walked towards the sun that was now hanging low in the western sky. Ahead, London could see where the land dropped off, the top of a hill he presumed. A split rail fence was ahead and it stretched away to both sides for as far as he could see. There was no gate but the four climbed over with no difficulty. It was about then that London realized what he was seeing.

In the distance, uncountable miles away the mountains went on while immediately in front of him was a sheer drop of thousands of feet. It was as though the ground had been cut off, straight down. Now he understood the term "end of the world." Here everything ended, only to start again far away as though it was the beginning of another land.

London stood and stared. No words could describe what he saw and felt. The spectacle of nature was overpowering in its beauty. His three hosts looked from the view to London and back again, making no sound and allowing him the rapture of the moment.

After a few minutes of wonderment, London turned to the others and said, "This must be one of the most beautiful places on earth. Thank you all for letting me see your Escarpment."

"Let's sit here and talk for a while," Roll said. "We got more than an hour before it gets full dark."

The four sat on the sun-warmed ground and Roll went on with his story.

"When we first got here there were twelve of us. A colored man and woman along with their child that we had bought in St. Louis and given their freedom if they would accompany us on the trip. Plus four men who were hired hands and two indentured women."

"That's eleven," London interrupted. "I thought you said there were twelve?"

Father, mother and daughter smiled together as Helen said, "Colleen was born just three months after we arrived so we consider her a charter member here at the ranch."

"But to get on with the story," Roll said glancing meaningfully towards the setting sun, "we have developed a rather unique community here and because of that, we have some rather unique rules."

"We have one guest house here at the ranch and that is where you'll have to stay for the night." Roll said. "You'll find it rather unusual in that it doesn't have any windows and only one door. All temporary visitors are required to be in the house from sunset to sunrise, no exceptions. After you've been here a few days and we have had more time to talk, maybe things will change. I certainly hope they will for all our sakes."

"Are you saying I'll be locked up for the night?" London asked.

"That's the rules." Roll said. "Even if Christ himself came riding in, he would have to spend the night time in the guest house with the door locked."

"This all sounds mighty mysterious," London answered. "I ain't sure I like being locked up, even if it is friends who are doing it."

"Well, it's the rules and we all have to abide." Roll said. "In time it will be clear to you why we do things this way but for now you'll just have to go along with our programs. I hope you're not offended."

London pursed his lips and looked at his three hosts. After a few seconds he smiled and said, "If it was anyone else who tried to lock me up there would be a BIG fuss before the job got done but since it's you, I'll go along and wait to hear what the reasons are going to be."

"Thank you, London," Roll said sincerely. "I appreciate your trust and I assure you that in the end you will understand. Now I'll walk you up to your cabin and make you as comfortable as possible for the night. Tomorrow I'll finish my story about the settlement here and things will be a bit clearer."

As Roll started walking away from the edge of the Escarpment, London looked back towards Helen and Colleen and said, "For the chance of meeting you two ladies and seeing the view from your front yard, a night in jail doesn't seem all that high a price."

They parted with a burst of laughter as London accompanied Roll towards a house at the far end of the settlement.

The small house that Roll walked towards was much more than

the rustic log cabins London was accustomed to seeing in the wilderness. It had a split shingle roof and a small porch in the front. The lap siding was cedar and painted white. As Roll had said there were no windows and only one door which was solid. A large brick chimney extended up one side indicating a fireplace.

Roll climbed the three steps, walked across the front porch and opened the door. Inside it was all one room, about twelve feet by twenty feet and very well appointed. There were two large chairs with thick cushions on the seats and backs. The hand polished cedar board walls gleamed from the glow of two large, coal oil lamps that were already burning in the room. One lamp rested on the mantel at the fireplace and the other set in the middle of a small table along the wall. There were two straight chairs at the table. A large bed nearly filled one end of the room, its heavy down mattress looking deep and comfortable. A luxury suite that was to be London's cell for the night.

Roll walked to the table and indicated a pitcher of fresh milk and half an apple pie, a bedtime snack.

"I can't stay now," Roll said, "'cause there's evening chores that need attending to. You should be comfortable enough here but, like I said, you won't be able to come out until morning. There's a chamber pot under the bed. One of the young'uns will be by in the morning to clean up so don't worry about that."

"I'm sure I'll be comfortable," London said as he sat tentatively on the edge of the large bed.

Roll reached out and rested his hand on London's shoulder as he said, "I'm ever so glad you came, old friend. I'll see you in the morning," and he went out the door.

London was not surprised when, as soon as the door was shut, there was the sound of a heavy bar falling into place and as he crossed the room and pushed on the door found it securely locked from the outside.

London pulled off his boots and brought one of the kitchen chairs over in front of one of the big easy chairs where he sat and rested his stocking feet on the impromptu footstool. More and more curious, he thought, running the events of the last few days through his mind. A dozen anvils, more plows than a man could use in a lifetime, Indians that spoke perfect English, guards in the woods, and locked up for the night were just some of the mysteries. And last but not least, the old man had been right. He had not seen a single outhouse.

Now he had Colleen to consider. She was undoubtedly the most beautiful woman he had ever seen and here she was in the middle of nowhere and was, of all things, a 'Doctor.'

London tried to relax and finally succeeded by thinking back to the sunset he had seen from the edge of the Escarpment. The most beautiful thing he had ever seen … maybe not quite. With visions of Colleen in his head he dozed off right there in the chair.

London woke with a start. One of the lamps had gone out and the inside of the cabin was dim. He was momentarily disoriented and his first reflex was his right hand slapping against his right hip where holster should have been. No gun. He snapped back and realized where he was. He stood on wobbly legs, his knees shaky because of the uneven support from resting his feet on the kitchen chair. He moved to the door and again checked, finding it still locked from the outside. On the floor beside the door was his bedroll and saddlebags. Opening both sides of the bags, he took a six-gun from each compartment and carried them to the table against the wall. Removing both weapons from their soft cloth wrapping he immediately checked that both guns were loaded and able to function. Tucking one of the identical weapons in his belt he crossed the room and lit the light on the mantel that had gone out. Now the room was brighter and he felt more at ease.

What the hell have I gotten myself into, he wondered? Are these people what they claim or have I walked into more danger than I can imagine? Why did I go along with being locked up? Is it just for the night or am I in here to stay? And what's going on outside that they don't want me to see or know about? All I really know about Roll Jacobs is what he has told me. All the information I picked up in town was more confusing than anything else. For all I know these people are leftovers from the Donner party. London smiled at this last and thought. That would sure make breakfast an interesting proposition.

He walked to the table where the pie and milk awaited his pleasure and sat down, picked up a fork and started on the pie, shaking his head to rid himself of all the craziness he had been thinking.

I guess it's being confined that is causing me to be so suspicious, he thought. I haven't been confined since Andersonville and thinking back to that is enough to give anyone the creeps.

London finished the pie and milk and undressed for bed. He placed both of his handguns on the nightstand next to his bed, took a deep breath and resigned himself to whatever the future might bring. His mind drifted to Colleen and he went to sleep in the deep feather bed with a smile on his face.

Chapter 5

London awoke to a banging on the door and he quickly pulled his jeans on over his obligatory long underwear and walked across the room. The door was slightly ajar and when he pushed it open he found two young boys about ten years old standing on his threshold. Between them sat a huge wash tub of water steaming a cloud into the cool morning air.

"We brung you your bath, Mr. London," the first boy said only to be immediately corrected by the second boy who said, "brought, not brung. You know Miss Deborah Ann said we was supposed to use good English."

London was surprised to see that the second boy was a young Indian, dressed the same as the first boy, who was white.

With the door now open each boy grabbed a handle on opposite sides of the tub and carried it into the house. The first boy went to a concealed handle near the fireplace and raised up a circular section of the floor. Underneath was a metal grate set two feet below the floor's surface. The boys lowered the tub into the hole that was a few inches larger all the way around than the tub. The Indian boy darted back to the porch and reappeared with a small pail containing coffee and set it on the table.

"Here you are, Mr. London," the Indian boy said. "Mister Jacobs said to tell you to come down to the main house when you're ready. It's that one over there," he said, pointing out the door at a large house a couple of hundred yards away.

London saw that his spare shirt and jeans had been freshly washed and ironed and hung on the porch rail.

London picked up his clean shirt and jeans and carried them into the house and placed them along with his saddlebags on a chair next to the tub. He removed his pants and stepped into the hot water still wearing his long underwear. Inside the tub was a container near the top that held a bar of soap. To the amazement of the two boys, London lathered himself all over, washing his underwear right on his body. Then he stood and took them off, rinsed them in the tub and hung them over a chair.

London picked up the glass he had used for milk the night before and filled it with coffee. He put the glass on the second kitchen chair next to the tub, picked up his socks from the floor and got back into the tub, the knees of his long legs nearly touching his chest. He scrubbed the socks with the bar of soap and, after wringing them out, tossed them next to his underwear.

London reached into his saddlebags without getting out of the tub and pulled out a short bladed skinning knife. Using the soap for lather, he began scraping and rubbing his face alternating this procedure with sipping coffee until he could feel no more whiskers.

"Well boys, what'a ya' think?" he said as he drank the last of his coffee. "I suppose I better get dressed and go see how the rest of the world is getting along."

As he dried off to get dressed London looked at his gun belt and holster on the floor by the door. He wondered if he should wear it. Up to now everyone he had seen around the settlement had been unarmed except for the boys with the rifles at the head of the valley. He knew he would appear out of place with his gun belt and revolver but the thoughts that had plagued him the night before still lingered in his mind. No gun, he decided. He would trust Roll and leave all of his gear on the front porch of his new residence.

London pulled on his clean jeans over his bare skin and hung his long underwear on the porch rail to dry. Then he rinsed out his other jeans and shirt and hung them next to his long johns. He pulled on his socks, wet but acceptable and put on his shirt and boots. Having a full head of hair that hung to his shoulders, he left his hat hanging on a peg in the wall and stepped out the door and headed for the main house, intentionally shortening his strides so the boys could march in step with their guest.

Roll Jacobs was standing on the porch of the biggest house in the settlement and came down the steps to meet London. Roll took London's arm and steered him towards a table that was under a canvas canopy near the flagpole, one of several canopies that had been erected since the night before.

"Good morning," Roll said. "How did you sleep?"

"Couldn't have been better," London answered. "And that bath you sent the boys over with was really nice. Hot water is a luxury that you never have on the trail. The bathtub inside the house is really something. Did you think of that?"

"That's just one of the little luxuries we have around here," Roll said. "But before we get to breakfast and more visiting, there's something I gotta' tell you."

"Has it got anything to do with all the tents you got set up?" London asked.

"Yeah, it does," Roll answered. "We're gonna' have some company today. Chief Ouseph of the Chopunnish Indians is coming here. You probably know them as the Nez Perce. Anyway, him and a bunch of his clan will be here around noon. Last night they camped in the trees back a ways and this morning they are getting fixed up for the visit. I swear them Indians, men and women alike would put our white women to shame when it comes to getting dressed up to go out and about."

"Must be a bunch coming," London said. "You got enough tents and tables set up for a passel of folks."

As they walked into the shade of one of the sideless tents and sat down at a table that would seat at least eight people, London saw that there were six tables under each canopy and five canopies that had been erected around the flagpole.

"I don't rightly know for sure but I figure over a hundred of them and about the same of us residents. This is the yearly exchange day and it's a big time for all of us," Roll said.

"You mean you do a lot of trading?" London asked.

"Yeah, in more ways than one," Roll answered as he reached over and ruffled the hair of one of the two boys who were still keeping close watch on London. "This boy here," he said indicating the Indian boy, "will be going back home. He and half a dozen Indian young'uns have been staying with us for the last year."

"A year!" London exclaimed. "Isn't that a long time for a visit?"

"Not really," Roll said. "You see back when I had only been in the valley for a short time, Chief Ouseph would come around once in a while to make sure everything was okay and we got to be friends. Over the years we have done a lot of favors for each other and about the fifth year we had the idea of trading kids off for a year. Some of his came to live with us and some of ours go to live with him. It has made any cultural differences seem insignificant and has pretty much put an end to the language problem. At that age the kids easily pick up the language of the people they are around."

A big smile creased London's face as he solved one of the mysteries that had been puzzling him. "Well that explains what happened to me on my way up here. I was riding along and I saw half a dozen Indians near the trail. I wasn't exactly sure how to behave but the people in town had said the Indians in this area didn't bother strangers as long as you minded your manners, so I just waved and said 'Good morning'. One of the Indian boys answered me in perfect English. I was so surprised I just stopped and stared as they rode off."

"Yeah," Roll said. "That could have been the advance party for the Chief. Sometimes he'll send a group ahead to set up the campsite for when he arrives. I think you'll find these Indians to be exceptional. And here comes some other company." Roll was looking over London's head back towards the house as he spoke.

Helen and Colleen were approaching, Helen carrying a coffeepot and a handful of cups while Colleen had a large tray with London's breakfast on it.

Colleen set the tray in front of London and said, "Good morning.

We were beginning to wonder if you were ever going to get up. Pa finally sent the boys over so you would get your food before it got cold."

London looked down at four eggs, ham, fried potatoes, steaming hot bread with golden butter and strawberry jam. Definitely not Donner food, he thought with a wry smile.

"Don't pay any attention to her," Helen said cheerfully. "Every time a person comes in from the trail and gets into one of these good beds they always sleep long for a few days."

"I surely did sleep good," London said starting on his food while Helen poured coffee for everyone.

Should I say what's bothering me, he was thinking. Maybe the best approach to these puzzles is just to ask questions and see what happens.

Taking a sip of his coffee, London said, "But I was bothered a bit as to why it was necessary for you to actually lock me in that cabin last night. It did seem a little strange."

"Well, we got our rules here at the Escarpment," Roll said. "Like I was telling you last evening there is good reasons for each and every one and after you been here a while you'll understand a lot better. We just all gotta' abide."

"Maybe you better tell me now so as I don't get into trouble. Not knowing the rules is kind of a worry to me," London said making it clear by his words and tone of voice he didn't like being kept in the dark and was expecting honest answers.

Helen and Colleen turned their eyes towards Roll waiting for his reply.

London noticed the slight hesitation and studied the faces of his three hosts trying to discern what was being left unsaid.

"Well," Roll said, "let me say this. There is nothing for you to be concerned about. For now let's just have our party with Chief Ouseph and his people. Later you and I will sit down and go over the reasons for those few rules we have here at the Escarpment. Soon you will understand why we do what we do."

"Truthfully I was hoping for a little more details," London said, "but for now, you're the boss. I'll wait but I think we should have that talk before very long."

With this last statement London felt he was being as adamant as he could be without being impolite.

"Now," London went on changing the subject abruptly enough to show he was somewhat unsettled, "I got someone to thank for washing up my spare clothes and sending them over. I've never been treated so nice since I can't remember when. And I haven't smelled so good in a long time either."

Helen spoke up and said, "We got a laundry house and it wasn't no bother to throw your things in with the others. Here we all live like a big family and everyone's got a job. Cook, carpenter, smith, farmer or cowboy, everyone does what they're good at and we all benefit."

"And you're a doctor?" London said looking at Colleen. "I think I'd like to hear a little more about how you came up with that job?"

Roll interrupted by saying, "I was just telling London about Ouseph's visit today and how the exchange with the young'uns works."

Once again London noticed he didn't get his question answered.

"Now, where did we leave off in our talk last evening?" Roll said, making a permanent change in the subject of the conversation.

"You had arrived here and were starting to set things up," London responded.

"The first year was pretty rough. We weren't really short of food so we concentrated on getting some houses built and fixing up corrals and pens for the animals. Not knowing what to expect at first we built everything in a half circle with the Escarpment on one side, a defensive position, just in case of trouble. The Choppunish ... Nez Perce ... showed up in the fall and were helpful in supplying us with buffalo robes for everyone and a half dozen of their beautiful horses."

"Why did they do this?" London asked, hoping to get an answer for a change. "Didn't they feel like you were imposing on their land."

"No, not really," Roll answered. "They never stay for any period of time here in the valley, mostly just pass through. They consider this area to be kind of a ... a ... medicine country. The Land of the

Rumbling Hills is what they call it."

"Why's that?" London asked.

"Far to the north," Roll said pointing in that direction, "is a volcano. Sometimes it smokes and rumbles a bit but we're sure that it's too far away to give us any trouble, right girls?"

Both women started to talk at the same time, obviously ready to voice their strong disagreement with Roll's statement.

"You know we have talked about this ..."

"Dad, I've told you a thousand times that the danger ..."

They all four started to laugh. "As you can see," Roll said, "we don't always agree about everything around here."

"I'm glad to see that you're only human," London said.

"But to get back to the story," Roll went on, "by the start of the second year we were getting the houses finished and set up shops of sorts to make a lot of the things we needed. Helen and I had been raised around engineers all our lives and we managed to start making this a comfortable place to live."

"Another wagon train got lost and three of the wagons decided to stop here and build their homes. Two of the families were Italian immigrants and the other was from France. The children, as they were born grew up multi-lingual in French, Italian, Spanish, English and Polish, The last two coming from our forth year arrivals."

Helen interrupted at this point. "He makes it sound like it was all fun around here. Well I can tell you that we worked eighteen to twenty hours a day, every day for years. And what with having a baby every year or so, I did my part, something he hasn't seen fit to mention just yet," and she gave her husband a mock scowl that had the sting taken out of it by Colleen's laugh.

Three men approached the group, politely interrupted, and Roll immediately introduced them to London. They were all tanned and sturdy, clean shaven and dressed in new jeans and freshly pressed flannel shirts. All were middle aged but the similarity ended at that point.

"These are three of our early arrivals," Roll said. "This short fellow here is Sean McNamara originally from Ireland and mostly a quiet man with a huge temper inside him that seldom comes busting out—anymore, that is."

London stood and extended his arm and watched his hand disappear into the huge paw at the end of the short man's arm. Undoubtedly the biggest hand he had ever seen on a man of that size.

The second man was introduced as Henri Merroux, a tall, slightly built man of French descent and London found his grip to be firmly polite but not overpowering and his manner was very sincere.

The third man was Peter Digondo. A short, feisty Italian who quickly shook hands and then impatiently started talking in excited tone, part English and part Italian. London understood only that there was some disagreement in the kitchen among the women about what was to be served for the afternoon meal and Roll was expected to sort out the problem.

"Excuse me for a few minutes," Roll said to London, "but I'm wanted in the kitchen. Helen and Colleen will entertain you for a few minutes and I'll be back as soon as I can," and he walked off with the other three men.

"Let me tell you about those three," Helen said. "The first man, Sean, is our best carpenter. He spends most of his time in the sawmill back at the tree line. Henri works mostly with horses and spends his time around the corrals and horse barn. The third man, Peter, is a boot maker and part-time tailor. He makes the most beautiful boots you have ever seen. About everybody has a pair for dress-up but they only wear the boots on special occasions like today. If you watch this afternoon, you'll see what I'm talking about."

"The way you explain it everyone around here has just one job," London said.

"No, not exactly," Helen went on. "It's just that everyone seems to have one thing that they are better at. Hunting, fishing, butchering, gardening or whatever, each person has found their own special place. Of course, each family has it's own way of life separate from everyone else. We're just like a very small town where everybody helps when the need arises."

Colleen added, "The best example would be that Sean would put a new roof on Henri's house in exchange for getting a horse broke to ride. You see what we mean?"

"For the most part I understand," London said, "but don't the people ever disagree?"

"Of course," Helen said, "but never to any great extent. The people who live here are more than just satisfied with their lives. They have all lived in other places and they realize what a wonderful place this is."

"And the children," London asked, "what about them?"

"Let me answer that, Mother," Colleen said. "Many of us have left for one reason or another and everyone has always come back."

"Do you mean that that everyone who has settled here or been born here is still here? No one has ever left?" London asked.

"With only one exception, that's true," Helen said

"What was that exception?" London asked.

"Oh, it was insignificant," Helen said. "Roll will probably tell you about it sometime."

London filed another evasion away for speculation.

Colleen spoke quickly in such a way that London suspected she had caught the puzzled expression on his face and was hoping to gloss over the unanswered question. "If you don't mind, Mother and I are going to help the other women with the preparations. Why don't you take the boys and walk down to the horse barn and look over the stock. You should enjoy checking out our remuda."

London stood quickly and gave a slight bow, realizing he was being dismissed and said, "Ladies, I will see you directly," and in the company of the two boys headed for the distant barn and corrals.

When he reached the barn, the first thing London did was check on his own horse. He found him in a stall with plenty of fresh water and the residue of corn and oats in his feed box. The barn, as was the case with all farms, was built into a hillside to allow ground level entry to the lower level for the animals and the upper level for feed, wagons and other supplies. It was a first class building, tight siding, smooth working doors and a solid roof.

Running down the side of the hill was a small stream and it was fenced off from the animals until after it had passed under a small locked room in one corner of the barn. Where it emerged from under the building it flowed through one corner of the corral where it fed a couple of troughs and continued through the pastures until it disappeared towards the Escarpment.

Several pairs of Percheron draft horses were in the corral, most likely a legacy of Henri Merroux's French influence. In the pasture spreading away to the rail fence which guarded the edge of the Escarpment were the rest of the horses, most of which were of the Appaloosa strain.

As London and the two boys climbed into the upstairs of the barn London thought he would see if the boys were any more adept at answering questions than the adults had been.

"What about that red flag that's flying down by the houses?" London asked the boys.

"Didn't Mister Jacobs tell you?" the Indian boy said. "Well it …"

The second boy interrupted immediately by answering, "It's just something that Mister Jacobs does. He'll tell you how it works, I'm sure. Now we gotta' get back to the house where you stayed last night and clean up. Cum'mon," he said to the Indian boy, grabbing his arm, and as they walked away, London could see one boy talking quietly but intently to the other boy.

Now what the hell could be secret about a flag, London thought. And another thing, the kids are as closed mouth as the grown-ups. I'm getting nowhere fast finding out what this place is all about.

As London started his walk back towards the houses, he heard some shouting and up ahead, saw a number of people mounting horses and beginning to ride up the valley. Looking that way he could see a large group of riders coming from the tree line and even at that distance he could make out that they were dressed almost entirely in white. It must be the Indians, he thought, unconsciously increasing his pace to reach the houses before they did.

He need not have worried because he reached the flagpole and the picnic area well in time to see the visitors come riding in.

Contrary to any other Indians he had ever seen on the move, they were all mounted on their beautiful horses, men, women and children alike. And there appeared to be no particular status beyond the fact that one man rode in the front center of the group. London guesses the size at well over one hundred individuals.

The first thing that impressed London, as the Indians got close, was their dress. Almost without exception they were wearing white buckskin. Pants, jackets, dresses, leggings, moccasins and headdresses; they were spotless and hand decorated with feathers and beads.

The weapons they carried were strictly ceremonial with the lances, bows and staffs decorated in the same manner as their clothing. The horses were brushed and combed until they positively glowed in the noon sun, a truly beautiful entourage.

And their attitude matched their attire. They were all happy and laughing as they greeted the people of the Escarpment.

Roll himself approached the now thoroughly mixed group of ranchers and Indians and made his way to what was obviously the leader of the Indian band.

London walked into the crowd and made his way close enough to hear Roll call out, "Hello friend, and welcome," to the distinguished looking Indian who sat his horse so easily.

"Ho, friend Jacobs, it is good for me to see you again," the Indian said as he swung his leg across his mount and slid softly to the ground. "It is a good day."

"Whenever friends meet it is a good day," Roll said as he guided Chief Ouseph to the shade of the tent while he beckoned London to come over.

As London joined the two men, Roll said, "Today we have a stranger in camp. He is an old friend to whom I owe much. He is called London and I have spoken to you of him."

London approached the Chief, not sure of exactly how to greet him but this was quickly solved as the Chief extended his hand and said, "I am pleased to meet a man who is friend of Jacobs."

London sized up the Chief as they shook hands, looking deep into the Indian's eyes. Ouseph looked back, his eyes momentarily squinting as London felt the Chief's scrutiny.

London found the Chief's hand to be small and fairly soft but with a strong grip and London said, "I am very pleased to meet the Chief of the great Chopunnish. You have a very beautiful people."

This was just the proper thing to say and the Chief, who had personally inspected every individual in his band, smiled proudly that his efforts had not been in vain.

Ouseph turned from London to Roll and said, "I must make mention of this at once as it may require you to act. There is a man hiding back in the trees unseen by your guard"

London heard the word 'guard' and paid closer attention.

"He is a small, old white man riding a sturdy mule," Ouseph said. "He watched us ride in and now remains back in the tree line. We did not interfere with the man preferring that you should handle him."

"We had a man like that come to camp a while back, an old prospector," Roll answered. "Could I use a couple of your people to go with Henri and Josh and show them where this man is? I'll have them bring him back here and we can get this straightened out ... again."

"Of course," Ouseph said and he shouted two names across the compound and a young man and woman quickly guided their horses to where he was standing.

Roll also shouted for his son Josh to join them and to bring Henri with him. Roll explained what he wanted done and the two men grabbed their horses from the hitching rail and just that quick the four were headed up the valley at a gallop on their errand.

London spoke up and said, "That could be the old man I was talking with in town. I don't think he likes you very much. He said he had been here a while back and that you had sent him on his way."

"Yeah, we did," Roll said. "He wanted to prospect in the mountains around here but the Chief and I decided to discourage this enterprise. We always just ask outsiders to move along and if they don't, we kind'a help them along if you get my meaning. But now, back to the party. Come on you two," and Roll put his arms around the shoulders of both of his friends. "Let's see what there is to eat."

Much thought and discussion had gone into the food that was to be served. There was no wild game except grilled trout. The meat was ground up beef, beef liver fried in huge skillets and roast pork. The side dishes were what the settlers had all the time but what the Indians considered great treats, potatoes, cabbage, cucumbers, beets, roasting ears and watermelons along with every kind of fruit pie imaginable. Gallons of cold tea and hot coffee were on the tables. People scattered in mixed groups all around, eating, talking, laughing and renewing old friendships and making new ones.

Three hours had gone by since the riders had left to go up the valley and London and Roll had taken turns walking around the houses watching for their return. London's younger eyes picked up the search party first and he called to Roll that riders were coming in.

Roll walked out from under the canopy and joined London. Helen and Chief Ouseph were at his side. They could make out the four that they had sent out and a fifth rider on a mule. As the party got closer, what they had speculated about earlier proved to be the truth of the matter. The trespasser was indeed the old prospector from town.

Roll walked away from the group, motioning them to stay behind and he met the riders about a hundred yards out. Henri and Josh, with the old man following headed for the cabin where London had spent the previous night. They walked him inside and after a couple of minutes came back out, barring the door from the outside.

London walked to where Roll was now standing and asked, "Looks like I'm gonna' have a roommate tonight, huh?"

Roll shook his head and kicked a stone with the point of his boot. "This old fart is getting to be a real pain in the butt." Roll studied London's face intently for a few seconds and then said, "You'll have to excuse me for a few minutes. There's something I got to talk to Helen about."

London watched with interest as Roll gathered his wife and headed for their house, Roll talking excitedly, as he motioned with his hands and bobbed his head.

London wandered back to the festivities as he mulled over what he had just seen. He drifted through the park like area looking for Colleen and found her sitting on a blanket with a small group of Indians and local residents. The Indians were a man and two women, in their twenties and a man and woman resident of similar age. Plates, silverware and scraps of food were in a stack beside their large blanket, residue from their lunch.

They all looked up as London approached and Colleen immediately jumped to her feet to make the introductions.

"Everyone," she said, "this is my father's good friend, London," and she took his hand and began indicating the people on the blanket.

"This couple here are Carolyn and Tom Kelly, the most newlywed people in the valley."

Tom Kelly stood to shake hands and say, "Welcome and pleased to meet you." Carolyn smiled shyly from her seated position and said, "Hello, Mister London."

The next person introduced was a robust Indian girl with a flashing smile, dark hair cut in short bangs and impish good looks. London saw her appraise him unashamedly. Colleen said her name was Star.

She spoke immediately saying, "I must say that you are younger and better looking than most of the visitors we see in this area," and she extended her hand from her seated position forcing London to reach and bend in order to grasp it.

"Don't pay any attention to her," Colleen said. "She says things like that to all of the young men and she has most of them scared to death that she might be serious. If a man ever flirted back she would probably put on a buffalo robe and run for home."

London gave his best smile to Star and said, "Even a buffalo robe couldn't hide her spirit and beauty."

"Oh-Oh, Star, you better be careful. This looks like one man you

45

won't be able to intimidate," said the Indian man. "My name is Red Fox and this is my betrothed, Morning," and he rose and stretched out his hand.

"Very pleased to meet you," London said.

"Morning and Red Fox came to our camp a year before I went to theirs," Colleen said. "We spent two years straight together and have tried to see each other as much as possible ever since. Star is Red Fox's sister and as close as a sister to me."

London sat down between Colleen and Star, slightly amazed at the straightforward talk of the women. No subservient attitude here, he thought.

"What brings you to the settlement?" Red Fox asked. "It's not very often we get visitors who are so obviously welcome."

"I came to visit Roll but I just thought I would be seeing him and maybe his family," London answered. "I didn't expect to meet a whole town and all of its neighbors."

"What are your first impressions?" Star asked, staring inquisitively at London.

"First is the beauty of the place," London answered, "and second is the common use of English by everyone for communication. It's positively amazing to me," and he again told the story of seeing the Indians along the trail and being wished 'Good Morning' in return to his greeting.

"Yes," Red Fox said, "I was talking to a couple of the men you are speaking about. Only the boys understood your greeting and that was the reason they rode off so quickly. The men wanted to know what you had said but they didn't want to ask where you might have heard them."

"In regards to the language," Colleen said, "we have been speaking only English because of you. We feel it would be improper to speak Chopunnish when you wouldn't be able to understand."

"But there are a few things I don't understand," London said deciding to give it another try.

"Like what?" Colleen asked.

"Well, like being locked up from sunset to sunrise, why the red flag is flying, why nobody has ever left here, why Roll would buy such unusual supplies in town ... Oh, lots of things."

Colleen put her hand on his arm and said, "Just stay for a while and everything will make sense. In time Father will make everything clear. For now just relax and enjoy yourself, right folks?" And she indicated all the others on the blanket.

"In time it will all make sense," Tom Kelly said. "Now, we don't get much news from the rest of the world so how about you filling us in on your adventure getting here?"

"Okay," London said, "but it's not that much of an adventure," and he told the story of his life for the last three years.

When he finished, Star said, "Tell us again about life on the riverboats. That must be really exciting."

London talked on, answering many questions from the beautiful Indians and his understanding and friendship for all these people grew and eased his discomfort.

Roll walked up to the group on the blanket and said, "I didn't want to interrupt but I need to talk with London for a bit. Colleen, would you please join us?"

Roll walked them away from the group towards the fence along the Escarpment with London and Colleen close behind. At the fence he sat on the top rail and as the two joined him, he began to talk.

"There is something I've got to say," Roll said looking at London. "This is not the time or the place that I had in mind but some unusual circumstances have forced me to adjust my schedule."

"What is it?" London asked.

Looking London straight in the eye and speaking in slow measured tone, Roll said, "I would like you to stay here with us and become a part of our community. How would you feel about that?"

"I'm not sure I understand," London said. "How long a stay are we talking about?"

"I ... we ... Helen and I would like you to stay from now on and settle here," Roll answered.

"I don't know, Roll," London said. "I've been on the move pretty much since the war and settling down has its appeal but I'm just not sure. I could agree to stay for a while, maybe through the winter but next spring I might change my mind and want to move on."

Roll looked at Colleen who was listening intently to the conversation and then looked out over the Escarpment towards the distant mountains. He stood for at least a full minute deep in thought.

"Okay," Roll said with a sigh, "that'll have to be good enough. Now I'm going to tell you the rest of my story and put as much trust in you as I have ever put in a person from the outside."

"I mentioned that this is a unique community," Roll continued. "We have advantages and riches here far beyond anything found anywhere else in the world. Many of these things will be shared with you but others must be kept secret because of their unusual nature, at least for now."

"I guess I better start at the beginning," Roll said. "The red flag you see flying from the flagpole is a sign that there is a stranger in the valley and everyone is to observe certain rules. The machine shop is to be shut down, the houses are to be kept closed and no lights are to be lit until after the visitor is put up for the night. And particularly no loose talk about the settlement or our rules."

"We have made certain improvements to our homes and lifestyle that some people just wouldn't understand," Roll went on. "I am going to have Colleen take you on a full tour of our homes and outbuildings and when you're done, about dark, we will sit down again and I will answer any questions you might have. Now I'm going to get back to our Indian guests."

"Come with me," Colleen said. "I think you are going to enjoy this."

London followed expectantly as Colleen crossed the picnic area and took him to the main house, up the steps and through the front door. Half the people in the settlement saw them go and within a very few minutes the other half had been told.

Chapter 6

The house, at first glance, seemed little different from the cabin where London had spent the previous night. Then Colleen began showing him around.

"Look at the windows," Colleen said. "Double panes of glass, inside and out to keep the cold away. There are no huge stoves in every room with their dirt and mess. We heat and light things up this way."

Colleen stepped to a large chandelier and picked up a match from the table. Turning a small knob, she lit each individual globe. London was amazed to see the amount of illumination that spread through the whole room, even in the daylight.

"What is that?" he asked.

"It is a burning gas that Father has brought to all the houses. It comes from the mountains and is brought here in pipes buried under the ground the same as the water."

London looked down at the floor and then back to Colleen. "What do you mean, water?"

Colleen led him to the kitchen and turned the tap over the sink. Water, cold and clean came pouring out. "How about that?" she said.

"That's wonderful," London said, "but why are there two spigots?"

"Another marvel," she answered as she turned the second spigot. "Here, feel this."

London stuck his hand into the stream of water and immediately jerked it back. "I'll be damned, hot water. Now how does he do that?"

"We'll get to that," Colleen answered. "Now look in here," and she led the way into the bathroom. A huge metal tub at least six-feet long stood along one side of the room with two spigots mounted on one end like the ones in the kitchen sink. London realized immediately what he was seeing.

"My goodness, a hot bath any time you want one," he said.

"Yes and even more. Look at this," Colleen said.

Sitting in one corner of the room was a seat with a box-like structure under it. Colleen lifted the hinged top to reveal a bowl full of water under the apparent out-house seat. On the wall over the chair was a metal container about one foot square. Hanging from the box was a chain with a wooden handle on the end. Colleen pulled the chain and water gushed through a pipe and flooded through the box under the seat.

"Everything is carried off through a network of underground pipes out away from all the living quarters," Colleen explained.

"I've never seen anything like this," London said somberly.

"Now come along to the other rooms and you'll see some of the early developments," Colleen said.

What more could there be to see, London wondered as he walked down the hallway of polished cedar walls and carpeted floors.

Colleen led him into a bedroom and said, "This is one of the guest rooms although we don't get to use it often. Here is a touch that I especially like."

On the wall in three different places were goose necked fixtures with the same kind of small valve on the bottom as London had seen in the front room. Colleen again struck a match and lit a jet of gas that came from the fixture. A globe over the light made a pleasant glow in the room.

"The reason I like these fixtures so much is that they are solid gold," Colleen said. "When Father first started using gas for light and heat, he had so much trouble working the metal that he used the softest material he could find that would still tolerate the heat. Chief Ouseph and his people gave father all the material he wanted from their caches in the mountains. Now we use a steel alloy that he developed in the machine shop to make the fixtures. Better maybe, but not near as beautiful to look at."

"Then that's the reason he orders things like plows and anvils?" London asked.

"Of course," Colleen said. "People think he is trading with the Indians but he really wants to keep it a secret that he has his own smelter up here."

"Where is the smelter?" London asked.

"It's in the machine shop where the steam engine is that supplies the power for the other work shops. It has to be shut down when visitors are in the valley because of the noise and smoke," Colleen said.

"What about the Indians?" London asked.

"Father trusts them completely. They have been coming here since the first year we arrived and they've seen almost everything that we have done so there's no sense in trying to hide anything from them. Now let me show you Mother's room and Father's room."

There was no doubt in London's mind whose room they had walked into. Two of the walls were covered from the floor to the ceiling with bookcases and contained a marvelous collection of textbooks on military history, world history and huge maps of every region of the known world. The gaslights were all around the room to dispel any nighttime shadows. A large rectangular table occupied the middle of the room and it was covered with books, papers and an accumulation of study materials.

"Since West Point," Colleen said, "Father has tried to maintain his study habits as time permits. He is a great believer in education."

London looked at her carefully as he said, "I suppose his belief in education is what led to you being a doctor."

"Not at all. It was my choice but it required me to leave the settlement in order to study in Europe. It is nearly impossible for a woman to attend medical school in the United States. There is still a great deal of prejudice against women in this country," Colleen said emphatically.

London could hear the change in her voice as she spoke this last statement. This was a subject he would be sure to bring up again if it aroused such a passion in her. Seeing her bristle and sparkle was pleasing to his eyes. "Now," she said calming down as she continued down the hall, "here is Mother's room."

It was a corner room with windows around two sides, floor to ceiling. The flowery brocaded furniture was arranged in a circle conducive to visiting. Off to the side sat a full sized grand piano. Colleen tinkled the keys and said, "Obviously, Mother plays."

Now London and Colleen were on horseback, ending their tour. They had walked to the barn and corral where she had shown him the locked room where the pump was located that fed water to a holding tank on the high ground, which in turn supplied the settlement. Then they saddled horses and went to the sawmill, smelter, machine shop and power plant.

"Everything is absolutely ingenious," London was saying as they rode. "And to think that many of the innovations were your Mother's ideas is even more remarkable."

London got the reaction he had hoped for when Colleen stopped her horse and spoke sharply, a frown on her face. "Do you mean that you're surprised that women can think? I would have expected more from you. That attitude is what forced me to go to Paris for my training."

"No, that's not exactly what I meant," London answered. "It's just that everything is so new and different. Your Mother's plans for hot water heaters in the houses and inside toilets. The next thing she'll want to use steam for both power AND HEAT. A very unusual lady."

Colleen stared at London and immediately forgave his discriminatory statement. "What did you say? Steam for heat ... my god ... what an idea. I've got to talk with Father about this."

"I was just talking," London said. "I didn't mean to ..."

"But can't you see," Colleen replied. "Pipes carrying hot steam through the house, warming the air. Even cleaner than the burning gas. Cum'mon," she said impatiently, "we've got to get back and ask about your idea." She put her heels to her horse as she headed for the settlement at a gallop leaving London to try and catch up.

There was only an hour or so of daylight left when they reached the main house. A group of people stood on the porch including Roll, Ouseph, Henri Merroux, Josh and Red Fox.

They were all obviously agitated and Colleen said, "What's going on?"

"Bad news," Roll said. "The old prospector used a stone from the hearth in the cabin and knocked a panel out of the front door and got out. London's gear was still on the porch and he stole one of his six-guns and a rifle. Then he went in the back of Sean McNamara's house and took three of the biggest gold fixtures. Star saw him running from the back of the house headed for the barn and yelled at him. The old man shot at her and she backed off and came to me. Meantime he got a horse and took off headed up the valley. Miguel Sanchez, Tom Kelly and a couple of Ouseph's men are getting ready to go after him. It's not quite dark yet so Miguel will be able to pick up his trail with no problem."

"I'd like to go along," London said. "There could be trouble and they might be able to use me. My horse is fresh and besides I feel a little responsible since the man has my guns."

"I'm going too," Colleen said. "I hope they won't need a doctor but again, they might. I'll just grab my kit and I'm ready to go."

"All right," Roll said, "just be careful. We don't want anyone hurt by this man. Helen is fixing a pack to take along with food and water in case he gets past Zack."

London was back in his element as the six riders galloped up the valley. He had grabbed his extra six-gun from the porch and just shoved the revolver under his belt in the small of his back.

London had been told that Miguel Sanchez was an expert tracker so London allowed him to lead the way but he kept close behind so he could go quickly into the lead if there was trouble. London could feel the danger and he knew that he had the most experience of anyone in the group in this type of situation. Only the presence of Colleen and her proximity to danger made him uneasy.

There was little doubt where the man was headed. His tracks led straight up the middle of the valley to the pass between the mountains.

"He's running his horse pretty hard," one of the Indians said.

"Yeah," Miguel answered, "and he's near to half an hour ahead. I hope he doesn't cause Zack any trouble."

It was full dark when they heard two gun shots up ahead.

"That was a rifle," London called out. His experienced ear could easily tell the weapon from the sound of the shot.

"It came from about the tree line," Tom Kelly shouted.

Unconsciously the group increased their speed and twenty minutes later were to the guard's location.

"ZACK! ZACK!" Colleen yelled, "WHERE ARE YOU?"

"Over here," a voice called off to the left of the trail.

They all slid from their mounts and went towards the sound. Tom Kelly lit a lantern and ahead they could make out a horse and a man on the ground.

"I'm sorry," Zack said, "but the man got past me. That's the second time I messed up in the past two days."

Colleen was already bent over her brother and had started examining him by the light of the lantern. There was blood all over the front of his shirt and more from his mouth as he tried to talk. Ripping his shirt open they could see a terrible wound in the lower right side of his chest. As Zack breathed, bubbles and pinkish froth flowed from the wound.

London watched as Colleen rolled Zack slightly onto his side so she could see where the bullet had exited his body, exactly half way between his shoulder blades, the worst possible spot.

"Colleen, who all is with you? Is London here?" Zack asked as he squinted his eyes to see in the dark.

"Be still and don't talk," Colleen said as she busied herself trying to ease Zack's pain.

But Zack kept talking. "I heard a rider coming and I yelled for him to stop. He stopped okay but as soon as I rode up to him, he just shot me without a word. He looked like the man that they came and took in earlier. Was it?"

"You couldn't know," Colleen said. "He stole some things from camp and grabbed a horse and took off."

"Yeah, he was riding one of the Appaloosas. That's what sort of threw me," Zack said. "Sis, do me a favor and tell Pa …" And he died.

London walked to where Zack's horse stood and checked the animal. It was breathing hard and covered with sweat. "Tom … Miguel … look here," he said.

"He switched to a fresh horse," Tom said. "Now he'll be even harder to catch."

"Here's what I suggest," London said. "Tom, you stay here with Colleen and build a travois and get Zack back to the settlement. The four of us will go on and finish this business."

"Okay, if you think that's best," Tom answered allowing London to make the decisions.

London walked to where Colleen knelt on the ground and stooped down beside her. "I'm so sorry about your brother but there is business that needs finishing. You and Tom take Zack back and I'll be along as soon as I can."

Colleen looked at London with tears streaming down her face and said, "Get him, London. Be careful but go get that bastard."

London picked up the Henry rifle that was lying next to the body, checked to make sure there were shells in it and stepped onto his horse. Turning to the two Indian men and Miguel, he said, "Let's ride!"

It was about two hours after sunrise when they first saw the single rider up ahead. Immediately the two Indians, being the lightest riders, veered to the right and increased their speed slightly while staying out of rifle range. London and Miguel also stepped up the pace and soon the riders were in a triangle with the Indians riding parallel and the other two closing slowly from the rear. The chase had continued for more than an hour in this manner when suddenly one of the Indians broke into a gallop and charged in from the side.

When London saw this he knew now was the time and he pushed his mount for the final sprint. The old prospector, seeing that further flight would be futile, stepped from his horse and raised his rifle towards the charging Indian, his closest adversary.

Seeing this London aimed his rifle in the direction of the old man and levered off four quick shots causing the prospector to flinch and miss the Indian. The charging pursuer veered away and now the old man turned his attention to London.

With less than a hundred yards separating them London also dismounted leaving his exhausted horse behind and started walking towards the man on the ground. Four more shots fired by the man on the ground missed and now the rifle was empty. The man raised the six-gun and began banging away with it. London continued to walk towards the man.

With the revolver now empty the old man made no attempt to reload, just dropped it on the ground and said, "Don't shoot, I give up," and stuck his hands in the air.

"I don't think so," London said as he calmly raised his rifle and shot the man through the chest, killing him instantly.

London walked on to the dead man and stood looking down at the body. He used the toe of his boot to turn the man on his back and reached down and unbuckled his gun belt from the man's waist. Putting it around his own waist he cinched it tight. Picking up the revolver he expelled the spent cartridges and reloaded it before placing it back in the holster. The other three men sat on their horses back a ways and just watched.

Here lays another dead man at my feet, London thought. Even if I don't count the war, how many is this? Twenty at least. My god, how could a man lose count of something like this?

It had been Antietam that had made London into the shell of a soldier. After that battle he had lost all feeling for his fellow man and had just worked at survival from day to day. Only once had he and Roll spoken of the horror and London had learned that Roll had been on the staff of General McClelland, the Union Commander. It was there that London learned that soldiers were just so much expendable equipment that officers used to win a battle. Human life meant absolutely nothing.

Roll, on the other hand had told London that sending men to their deaths was just another duty that was expected of him and the slaughter of Antietam had torn the heart from his body.

Next had come Gettysburg where London had watched as his men cried tears as they shouted and begged the attacking forces of Pickett's Charge to go back ... retreat ... so they wouldn't have to shoot down any more.

Then the gun fights on the riverboats and protecting himself and his employer's money on the Texas frontier. And the three men in the poker game in Denver when he was on his way to the reunite with Roll.

London nudged the body again with his boot and thought, I'm nothing but a killer. That's all I ever was and all I ever will be. Can I ever be a normal human being able to live in peace with friends?

London walked away from the body and waited for Miguel and the two Indians to join him. He kicked some dried brush and grasses into a pile and sat down, lighting a small fire.

"Miguel, how's about getting that coffee pot and coffee out of that pack you're carrying and opening up a couple a cans of beans if you don't mind," London said. "It's been a long night and longer morning and I could sure use some food and coffee."

While the coffee brewed the four men hobbled their horses and the two white men pulled the saddles from the animals permitting them to rest and graze.

"Ho, London," one of the Indians said, "You have a very fine horse. Not many can keep up with our Appaloosas."

"Thank you," London replied. "You have fine horses also. Not many can keep up with my tall Texas horse."

They all laughed as much as a relief from the tension of the chase as anything else.

It was well after midnight when the four rode back into the set-tlement. They had stopped once more on the way back to rest the horses, fix a bite to eat and take a short nap. They slid from their mounts in front of the main house and were met instantly by Roll, Helen, Colleen, Josh, Star and Chief Ouseph.

"I'll take the horses," Josh said and headed for the distant corral with the sweat covered and weary animals.

Roll had noticed that London was wearing his gun belt and his own rifle was in the saddle scabbard. "Is everything okay?" he asked London.

"Yeah," London answered as he handed the bag with the three gold fixtures to Roll. "I sure am sorry about Zack."

"Me too," Miguel said as he handed Zack's rifle to Helen.

"And the old man?" Colleen asked.

"We buried him about a mile off the trail," Miguel said.

Chief Ouseph spoke to one of the Indian men who had been on the chase and the man answered the Chief in their native tongue. Everyone's eyes snapped towards London as Ouseph said, "This man said you did what needed to be done. He said you are a good man and we all should thank you."

London nodded to the Chief in acknowledgment of the compliment and said to Roll, "Now a little sleep would suit me just fine. Do you want me to stay in the cabin?"

"Not any more," Helen said. "Colleen will show you to the guest room and we can talk more in the morning."

"Come this way," Colleen said as the group broke up and everyone headed for a place to rest.

As Colleen led London down the hallway she said, "Dark Cloud said that you shot the man who killed Zack and I'm glad you did. Now get some rest," and she paused in the doorway, put her arms around his neck, and kissed him lightly on the cheek.

"Good night, London," she said as she turned and walked to her room.

London watched her until she was out of sight and then walked to his bed and pulled off his boots and shirt. He fell back on the bed. The thoughts of the kiss, still soft and moist on his cheek lingered as he pushed all of the recent happenings out of his mind. Within a minute he was sound asleep.

"I don't know what we're going to do with you," Colleen said from the doorway after awakening him with a loud knock. "You sleep later every morning."

"Sorry," London answered from his seated position on the side of the bed. "What's the schedule for today?"

"There's a hot bath waiting for you and then Father wants you to join him in his study room. Breakfast will be waiting for you there so if you don't want to eat it cold, you had better get moving. You'll find clean clothes waiting beside the tub."

He wanted to dally and enjoy the convenience of the bathroom but he dared not keep people waiting so London rushed through his bath and shave and joined Roll. Helen, Colleen, Chief Ouseph, Red Fox and Josh were all sitting around the big table with Roll when London arrived. One place had been set for breakfast and London sat down and started to eat. Everyone else had coffee from a big pot in the middle of the table.

Roll came right to the point. "The first thing I want to do is thank you again for handling the problem of the prospector. You did the right thing ... really the only thing you could do under the circumstances."

"I suppose so," London said noncommittally around a mouthful of food.

"Anyway," Roll went on, "we've been talking about the funeral arrangements for Zack. He'll be buried this afternoon in our cemetery up near the tree line. After that Helen would like for you to meet with her and Colleen to discuss a job they would like for you to start. Something well within your capabilities."

"Of course," London said. A sarcastic thought popped into his mind. I wonder who I will have to kill this time but he pushed it aside and went on with his breakfast

"Good," Roll said. "Now we all have a lot to do so I'm going to leave you here with Chief Ouseph to get acquainted and we'll see you in a couple of hours."

With everyone gone but the Chief, London wasn't sure how to open the conversation but Ouseph spoke first saying, "My men tell me you were very brave in facing the man with your guns."

"During the war I was in many battles," London said. "Sometimes there were many guns firing towards me but I was never hit. Just one man with one gun did not seem dangerous to me and besides I had met this man in town on my way to this place and knew him to be old. I believed that he did not have the young eyes of a sharpshooter."

"This may be so," Ouseph replied, "but still you rode far and well and faced the danger bravely. My people admire this in a man."

"Thank you, but it was just my duty," London said.

"Very well," the chief said changing the subject. "Would you tell me about your time in the Great War back in the east?"

London finished his food and moved to a chair beside Ouseph and said, "My first big battle was at Antietam. I had seen some action in smaller skirmishes but that battle changed me forever. The slaughter was terrible and it is difficult to explain because I never really understood the overall battle plan or the how and why of it. I know that Roll was there on the staff of the Commander of the Union forces. Roll was greatly disturbed by what he saw there and is reluctant to discuss it, even with me."

Ouseph rubbed his chin with one hand and said, "This surprises me. Roll and I have spent much time talking of the war and the strategies and he never mentioned he was at that battle."

"I know it was a difficult experience for him," London said. "We all have things we keep to ourselves. I feel much the same way about Antietam."

"Very well," Ouseph said, "but Roll tells me you were at Gettysburg. Are you able to discuss that battle?"

"Better than the other one," London said. "By that time I had been in the army for over two years and had become hardened to battle. I was a Sergeant by that time and in charge of an infantry platoon that was in support of the artillery at the north end of Cemetery Ridge."

"Here, I can show you," London said standing up and taking a book down from a shelf. "This shows the position of the forces."

Opening the book to a double page map, London indicated the north end of Cemetery Ridge where a curve in the defensive position prevented a flanking movement by the Confederate army.

"The Southern General Pickett chose to charge with his army across the open ground from Seminary Ridge and our position on Cemetery Ridge. For two days he had been observing our position and he believed that he had a full count of the rate of fire from our cannons on the hill. Pickett felt the forces he had under his command could attack and overcome the Union position. But the night before he attacked, unknown to his observers, the Union forces brought an additional fifty some cannons into the line increasing their fire by almost fifty percent."

Ouseph was studying the map with care as London talked, tracing with his finger the course of the battle.

"When the charge came," London said, "the Rebs marched into a slaughter but they just kept coming, rank after rank. The infantry units didn't do anything but watch as the cannons cut them down. At first they shot explosive cannon balls into the Confederates but as the attackers got closer the cannons switched to shot shells and chains completely decimating the ranks of the Rebs."

London paused in his narrative and looked down at the table, pulling himself together to finish the story.

"Towards the end of the charge the Union troops were shouting at the Rebs to go back, 'GO BACK ... RETREAT ... PLEASE ... GIVE UP ... DON'T MAKE US SHOOT ANY MORE' the defenders screamed at the attackers and finally the charge was broken. It was a bitter day for this country and something everyone who was there will never forget."

Ouseph looked once again deep into London's eyes and said, "Now I know what I saw in you the day we met. You were dead inside and for that reason I felt fear. I hope you will overcome these feelings and once more learn to live."

"Thank you," London said. "I hope time will make things better. Now tell me why these strategies of our war interest you?"

"Since the second year Roll was in this valley," Ouseph said, "Roll has been teaching me military history. We have spent much time going over his books and papers studying the great battles of the world. He says I have a natural understanding of tactics."

"Other than personal satisfaction you have no real reason for learning all these lessons?" London asked.

"Many wars have been fought between the red man and the white," Ouseph said. "The teachings of West Point that Roll has imparted to me could be very important to the future of my people. I hope there will never be trouble but I believe it is best to be prepared."

Now London studied Ouseph intently. "You are a wise man," London said. "What you have said is disturbing to me because it means someday we could become enemies. I don't believe I could ever face such a situation."

A noise in the doorway caused each man to look up. Josh was standing there and he said, "Excuse me but I got your horses outside and Pa would like for you to ride up to the sawmill with him."

Ouseph and London walked outside and mounted up. Roll was waiting for them a couple of hundred yards off in the direction of the sawmill and power plant.

When the three arrived at the shops the men stopped their machines. The spider web of belts continued to spin and flop even though they were no longer supplying power with the clutches engaged. With all the noise it was difficult to talk inside the building.

Roll pointed to Sean McNamara and indicated he wanted the coffin on a table carried outside to where a horse and wagon waited.

"SEAN," Roll shouted over the noise of the machinery, "will you come with us? We're going to the ice house and put Zack in the coffin and make sure he looks presentable before we take him down to the settlement."

With the coffin in the back of the wagon, Sean fitted the lid and then he and London climbed in and sat on the box to keep it from sliding around on the short pull up the hill. Roll drove the wagon with Ouseph on the seat beside him. All of the men who had been working in the shops came outside to watch the wagon make its slow way to the ice house, pick up its melancholy passenger and start back down the hill. Back at the mill London and Sean hopped down from the wagon with Sean going back to work until it was time for the funeral. London mounted his horse and leading the other two mounts followed the wagon back to the settlement.

There were at least two hundred people, settlers and Indians combined in the procession that headed towards the tree line and the cemetery. At the mill and power plant another dozen men joined the group.

London positioned himself behind the family and within an arms reach of Colleen as everyone stood around the grave. Roll and Henri read scriptures and spoke reverently over the coffin. Ouseph also stepped forward and spoke in his native language what was obviously a tribute to the dead. At the end the settlers and Indians joined in a chant before going back to English and singing a final hymn. As the people began to filter back down the hill, Josh, Red Fox and one other young Indian remained at the grave site with shovels.

Roll, Helen and all of their family walked in a group apart from the rest. Just a few steps down the hill Roll stopped and gently motioned for the rest of the family to go on without him. Turning slowly he walked alone back up the hill and continued on until he disappeared into the trees.

London, still standing near the grave turned to Josh and said, "Can I do anything?" while nodding his head in the direction of Roll.

"No," Josh answered with a deep sigh and tears in his eyes. Waving his hand to the grave he said, "We can handle this and I know Father just wants to be alone for a bit to collect his thoughts. Thank you anyway," and he turned to complete his awful ordeal.

London walked slowly back to the settlement alone with his thoughts. Dead is just dead but at least under these circumstances there was time to mourn and feel the pain of the survivors.

Back at the settlement London stayed within sight of Colleen but did not impose on her grief.

After about an hour Roll joined the group and, to all outward appearances seemed to be in full control of his emotions.

The Indians, London had learned, were staying for several days and were being billeted all over the settlement. The women were staying in individual homes and the men were sleeping in the barn and other out buildings. Tonight a number of young people, both settlers and Indians were planning on sleeping out at the tree line.

Food once again came from the cookhouse in abundance. Ham, chicken and the ground up beef made into fist size servings were the main meats. The assortment of fruits and vegetables were everything the region had to offer. The Indians favorite desert was fruit pie of every kind with apple being the most preferred.

London had developed a particular liking for the cold tea served with ice, drinking glass after glass until someone noticed and mentioned it forcing him to explain by saying, "Since you don't have any beer, this is the next best thing."

It was nearly dark and the campers had departed for the tree line and many others had gone to where they would be spending the night when Helen and Roll called to London and asked him to accompany them to Roll's study room.

They relaxed into chairs and Helen spoke first saying, "We want to talk to you about doing something for us."

"If I can," London answered compliantly.

Helen went on by saying, "Roll and I want you to write a history of this camp from the time the Indians named it the Land of the Rumbling Hills up until now. We feel that if one of us should try to write it the story would be flavored by our own personal prejudices. All the people in the camp and the Indians who have been involved will help you in any way they can. Also whenever Colleen's not busy in the clinic she will help you."

"How much do you want me to write?" London asked as his mind immediately centered on a problem. "For instance how would you want me to handle the situation like the old prospector?"

"At first," Roll said, "we should put everything down exactly as it has happened from the start of our journey in St. Louis right up until today. Later we can go over the manuscript and see if there are any compromises we should make."

"I've never done anything like this before," London said, "but I would be willing to give it a try. At least it will keep me from feeling like a freeloader."

Working with Colleen on this will also be welcome, London thought, not knowing that unbeknownst to him and Roll, that this had been Helen's plan all along.

"Another thing," Roll said. "We will be going to town in a few days to pick up supplies that the storekeeper is holding for us. It's always a kind of excursion for everyone who makes the trip. It'll take us at least three or four days each way, depending on the weather and this time Chief Ouseph and a few of his people want to go along. Josh and Colleen will be going and Henri Merroux will supervise the Percheron teams. And Peter is going along to drop off half a dozen pairs of boots at the store to see if they will sell."

"Are you going?" London asked.

"Not this time," Roll replied. "There's a project I want to start as soon as possible so on this trip Colleen will be in charge."

"Yeah, I think I'd like to go along," London said, "even if it's only to get a glass of cold beer. Your tea is good, but for me beer is better."

"Tell you what," Helen said. "If you do a good job writing our story we'll make a batch of beer right here in the valley. We already have all the ingredients so when you get back from town you can be our writer AND our brewmeister. What do you say?"

"Sounds great," London said licking his lips. He could almost taste the beer already.

"I do want you to check on one thing for me when you're in town," Roll said. "There is a kind of wire fence I would like to order and I want you to see if the storekeeper can get it."

"You don't mean barbed wire, do you?" London asked. "I saw a lot of trouble over that in the last couple of years."

"No ... No ...," Roll said, "I wouldn't have the stuff on the place. What I want is the four-foot high woven wire cattle fence. About the only fence we have is to keep the horses and milk cows contained except for the rail fence along the Escarpment because of the children. I just feel that the wire fence will be better than the split rail and will hold the animals better."

"When will we be going?" London asked.

"Early morning day after tomorrow," Roll said. "I know we all just went through a bad time but we can't let that interfere with living. The work must get done."

The next day was spent rigging the wagons and allowing the Indians to go to their base camp and return in their 'work clothes'. An hour after daylight on the following day the caravan set out. There were six wagons with a driver and passenger in each one and twenty riders, fourteen of which were Indians including Chief Ouseph.

On the night of the second day they camped not far from where the old prospector had been buried. During the day Colleen had driven one of the wagons and London had ridden as her passenger. He told her all the details of the chase and the demise of Zack's killer. When he spoke of shooting the old man he said it was something he owed her family and it was the only way to solve all of the problems.

"If he had been allowed to return to town with the gold fixtures or even the knowledge of them, the problems for the valley and the Indians would have been catastrophic," London said as he finished the story.

"Yes, I suppose so," Colleen said. "One thing I am sure about is that Father has a lot of faith in you. Not to have gone after the man himself for one thing and allowing the wagons to go to town while he stayed at the settlement for another. This is the first time anyone has ever gone after supplies without Father going along."

"You're the one in charge, not me," London said.

"Hey, fella'," Colleen said, "who's kidding who here. You know very well he's counting on you to … LOOK! OVER THERE! What's that?"

About half way to the tree line were three animals, one considerably larger than the other two. The outriders had already noticed and stopped to stare.

"Grizzly bears," London said. "It looks like a sow with a couple of cubs."

The wind was blowing from the bears towards the wagons and the horses, smelling the bears, were acting skittish. Ouseph who had been riding close to Colleen's wagon said to London, "These big bears are considered bad luck to my people. Some years ago when game was scarce they attacked our camps and killed many horses and even a few people. Most still hate and fear these animals."

"Do you want to try and kill them?" London asked the Chief.

"No. Not kill them but maybe we could chase them away," Ouseph said.

"I know just what to do," London said as he jumped down from the wagon and walked to his horse and removed his bedroll. He took out the two piece .22 rifle and assembled it. The bears were still several hundred yards away. London slipped a cartridge into the breech of the weapon and aimed high in an attempt to lob a bullet into one of the bears. He fired and one of the smaller bears squalled and woofed loudly. Then the sound of the shot reached the bears and the big female rolled her head back and gave a fearsome roar. Both of the young bears ran behind her as London fired another shot in their direction. London was rewarded with a loud growl from the big female and she immediately started for the tree line herding her young ones in front of her. Just to be sure London pulled his six-gun from his holster and fired three more shots into the air helping the bears to hurry along.

"There, that should teach them a little respect," London said, "and nobody's the worse for wear, even the bears."

"May I see your little gun?" Ouseph asked.

"It's good for small game like rabbits and prairie chickens," London said as he handed the gun to the Chief.

"I see. It is also light weight and the ammunition is small," Ouseph said. "Where can I get some of these?"

"The storekeeper in town told me he had some in stock," London answered.

"When we get to town will you get me some of these guns and the bullets that they shoot?" Ouseph asked. "It would be better if you bought them because the storekeeper might not want to sell them to an Indian. I can settle later with Jacobs for the cost."

London paused for a second too long so Colleen answered for him. "Of course," she said. "I know my Father would approve."

"Now if you will let me use this gun and some shells for the afternoon," Ouseph said, "we will have many prairie chickens for dinner tonight."

After Ouseph had ridden off, Colleen said, "Now there's a man who's not afraid to try something new."

"So I've noticed," London replied. "When I talked with him a couple of days ago I was amazed at his knowledge of military tactics. It's a shame that one of his sons can't go back east to West Point for an education but with slavery abolished the only people that are free to abuse are the Indians."

"I have the feeling that Ouseph and his people would be a bad group for anyone to pick on," Colleen said.

"This is true," London answered as he leaned back on the wagon seat and thought back over his conversations with Ouseph.

There was no doubt the Chief was a smart man and his continued contact with white men had given him considerable insight into the problems that could develop in this part of the west. Could it be, London thought, that Ouseph realizes that between the gold in the surrounding hill and mountains and the millions of acres of prime ground that someday he might have to fight to protect his homeland?

Could it be that Ouseph is already preparing?

London glanced at Colleen seated beside him. Could she one day be living in the middle of a war?

So many of his questions had been answered and now new problems had taken their place.

The afternoon wore on and London and Colleen chatted away. He didn't bring up his concern about the future of the Nez Perce as the wagon trains kept pouring people into the west. London decided it would be prudent to discuss this with Roll and get his opinion. Surely Roll had foreseen this situation and given it some thought. He would wait and see, London thought.

Up ahead there was a stream crossing the trail and a small copse of trees. London nudged Colleen and said, "It'll be dark in another hour or so. How does that look for a place to stop for the night?"

"You got it fella'," Colleen said. "These reins are starting to get heavy."

After eating, London had helped Henri look after the draft horses and found them to be in fine shape. Then he had joined the group of Red Fox, Morning, Star, Josh, Ouseph and Colleen on the ground beside one of the wagons.

London and Colleen sat with their backs against one of the huge wagon wheels and looked at the billions of stars in high, black sky. Occasionally they took part in the small talk but mostly they just sat quietly, enjoying the night. In ones and twos the others drifted off until they were alone.

Colleen got to her feet and said, "Don't say a word. Such a time doesn't need talk," and she climbed into the wagon leaving London and his bedroll to look at the sky alone.

Chapter 7

The arrival of the wagon train stirred quite a commotion. It was very seldom that more than three or four Indians came to town at the same time and, with all the rest of the caravan, it was a diversion that the townsfolk really enjoyed.

London was still riding with Colleen on the seat of the lead wagon. He looked around the town like he was returning to a well-known place. No changes, he thought and then smiled at himself. How many days has it been since I was last here? Just a little over a week. He gave a slight shake of the head and thought it seemed like weeks, months even, with all that had happened.

London hopped down from the wagon and looked back and at Colleen. "I'm going to keep the promise I made to myself," he told her.

"I think I know what that might be," Colleen answered. "I bet you're going to the saloon for a beer."

"Okay," she said smiling. "I'll be over at the general store making arrangements for the supplies. As soon as I'm done I'll join you for a beer."

"You're coming to the saloon?" he asked in surprise.

"Sure," she answered. "I like beer too. And don't start that 'but you're a woman' or you can drive the wagon home." With a slap of the reins she headed the horses towards the store.

London walked into the saloon and was instantly recognized by the bartender who said, "Looks like you found Jacobs."

"Yeah, I did," London answered. "How about a beer?"

"Sure enough," the bartender answered. "Have any trouble getting there?"

"Not a bit," London replied, picking up his schooner and walking to a table at the front window where he could keep his eye on Colleen as she drove to the store. He sat on one chair and rested his heel on another as he watched Morning, Star, Colleen and Henri enter the store. Colleen had a sheaf of papers in her hand, a list of the supplies she would be picking up.

London sipped his beer, enjoying it immensely. As he watched out the window he saw two men come riding into town and tie their two mounts and a packhorse to the hitching rail in front of the store that Colleen and the others had just entered. They were a rough looking pair. One tall, fat and dirty, the other was short but fatter and dirtier than the first. They were passing a whiskey bottle back and forth as they got off their horses and went immediately into the store.

London knew trouble when he saw it so he picked up his beer and drained the glass as he walked back to the bar. He dropped two half-dimes in front of the bartender and said, "I need a refill and would it be okay if I carry this glass over to the store for a minute? I want to check on something. I'll be sure and return your glass."

"Go ahead," the bartender said.

London picked up the full glass and went out the door headed for the general store. He got there just in time to see the fun start. London stopped inside the door and decided to watch for a minute.

The taller of the two men that he had seen ride in was holding onto Colleen's arm and she was saying, "How dare you say that! You call these two beautiful women 'dirty Indians'. You two filthy animals. Get the hell away from us!"

"Now that's what I like in a woman," the tall one said. "This'n here's got spunk and I like that red hair, too."

Colleen didn't struggle. She just stood straight, looking at her tormentor as she would view a run-over skunk.

London snapped the keeper strap from the hammer of his revolver and started to step forward when the storekeeper spoke up, saying, "Here now, leave that woman alone. If you can't behave yourselves get out of my store."

"Shadd'up you," the shorter man said. "This ain't none of your business."

London had taken one step when Henri Merroux walked between Colleen and the man who was holding her arm. "Gentlemen," he said, "I'm afraid I must insist. Stop bothering the ladies!"

"Insist this," the man holding Colleen's arm said as he let go of her and pulled a large knife from the back of his belt.

London nearly pulled his six-gun but what happened next was something to see. Henri leaned close to the tall man and as the knife came between them he lifted one foot from the floor and kicked the man's wrist effectively dislodging the weapon from his grasp. Then Henri's other foot came off the floor and he kicked the tall man directly under the chin. The man was unconscious when he hit the floor.

London started laughing at the way Henri had so easily handled the man but the second man was not amused. Turning his attention from the storekeeper to Henri, he made as though he was reaching for his pistol. He never should have looked away from the storekeeper. Almost before he knew it, he was looking into the muzzle of a double-barreled shotgun.

"Now," the storekeeper said, "you get your friend and drag him out of here before somebody really does get hurt."

"Excuse me ma'am," London said to Colleen surprising her at his sudden appearance. "If you would be so kind as to hold this glass of beer for me, I'll help this fella," and London indicated the short fat man with a nod, "get his friend out of here."

"Have you been there all the time?" Colleen said. "Why didn't you do something?"

"There wasn't nothing needed done. Looked to me like Henri handled everything just fine," London answered with a laugh.

Colleen was recovering her composure and her temper was falling from the violence range as she chuckled and said, "I guess you're right." She turned to Henri and asked, "What did you just do? I never saw anything like that in my life."

"That is savate," Henri said calmly, "something I learned in my youth but have never forgotten."

"Hey," the storekeeper hollered at the short, fat man. "Get your friend and get out'ta here!"

London handed his beer to Colleen. "Here, let me help. You get the heavy end and I'll take this end," he said as he gathered both of the fallen man's pants cuffs into one hand. "This is the easiest way to carry."

As they were going out the door, Colleen turned to Henri and said, "That was wonderful. I never knew you had such a talent."

"It is something I seldom use on the horses," Henri answered with a laugh.

There was a watering trough in front of the saloon and that was where London dropped his end of the heavy load.

"What say we throw a little water on your friend?" London asked. "Maybe we can get him to walk inside for a beer instead of being carried?"

"Sure would be better than toting his sorry ass any farther," the other man said as he dipped his hat in the horse trough and poured the water into his friend's face.

Spitting and sputtering, the half-drunk man sat up and looked around. "What the hell happened?" he asked.

"Some skinny guy over in the store kicked the shit out'ta you," his friend answered. "This guy here," and he indicated London, "helped me carry you over here."

The man got up from beside the watering trough and said, "Well, whoever he was he ain't gonna' get away with that. I'm goin' back to the store and settle with him."

"What, and turn down a free drink here in the saloon?" London said, patting the man on the shoulder.

"Free drink?" the man responded. "Who's buying drinks?"

"I am," London answered, "cum'mon inside."

The two dirty men navigated the stairs and went through the swinging doors with no problem and quickly bellied up to the bar.

"Give these two what ever they're drinking," London said, "and give me another beer."

As the bartender poured whiskey for two and drew a beer for London, he said, "You didn't lose my glass did you, Mister London? You said you'd bring it back."

"No, it'll be along soon enough. A pretty lady will be returning it to you in just a little bit," London answered.

"Hey, looka' there," the tall troublemaker said pointing out the front window of the saloon. "Another Injun."

Chief Ouseph had ridden up and was getting off his horse across from the saloon.

The man pulled his six-gun from it's holster and started waving it around as he said, "I'm gonna' have me some fun and see if I can make that there Injun across the street jump some."

"No, don't do that," London said. "He's not bothering you and I don't want you to be a bother to him."

"Who the hell are you to be tellin' me what to do?" the man said staring hard at London.

Already the bartender had retreated to the door of the kitchen ready to escape out the back when the shooting started.

London spoke calmly as he said, "That man happens to be an Indian Chief and besides that he's a friend of mine. If you try to take a shot at him, I'm going to stop you."

The tall man was glaring at London while he made up his mind where to point his revolver when his friend stepped in front of him and spoke to London.

"Did I hear the bartender call you Mister London?" he asked.

"Yeah, you did," London answered.

"Was you in a gun fight at a gambling joint in Denver this spring?"

"Yeah, I was," London answered again.

"Oh, shit," the short man said as he turned to his friend. "This here is the guy I was tellin' you about from Denver. He went up against three men over a poker game. He killed all three and only one of them even got his gun out'ta his holster. Come on, Ed, let's get the hell out of here."

The tall man allowed himself to be led away and London watched out the window as they went to their horses, mounted up and rode out of town.

About an hour later London walked back over to the store and found the men from the settlement out front loading the smaller and lighter supplies into the wagon that was parked there. Behind the store the bigger and heavier items were being loaded into the rest of the wagons. London found Colleen inside checking her list against the store's inventory. Her beer glass was sitting on the counter and London went to pick it up.

"Hey," the storekeeper said. "Maybe now you can answer a question for me, Mister London?"

"What's that?" London asked.

"Did you find out what Roll Jacobs wants with all those plows and anvils?" the storekeeper asked.

"Yep," London said as he turned and walked out the door.

"Well … Hey … Fella … Wait a minute," the storekeeper was saying.

London never paused or looked back.

Colleen was again driving the lead wagon and London was riding beside it on his horse.

"Did you get everything you went after?" he asked.

"Yes we did," Colleen answered. "Except for the fencing, that is. The storekeeper is going to order it in and we'll pick it up on the next trip to town."

"What about the guns for Ouseph?" London asked.

"He had three in stock so I bought them and all the ammunition he had," Colleen said.

"How do you pay for all this stuff?" London continued with his questions.

"About once a year father goes to Denver and draws gold coins from his bank there. Everything in the bank is in four names. His,

Mother's, Josh's or mine. Just in case of an emergency or whatever."

London swung his horse close to the wagon and jumped from one to the other. He tied the reins to a rope on the side of the wagon and settled onto the seat next to Colleen.

As she drove he sat and studied her profile. Was it all the time he had spent alone that influenced him or was she really the most handsome woman he had ever seen? He knew she was aware of his scrutiny but never once did she glance at him. Although he had only known her for a week, he was beginning to think she was as near to perfection in a woman as he had ever seen.

So, what does all this mean, he thought? Could it be a fact that she would never be allowed to leave the settlement? That was what Roll had said. If so, what would he do in the spring? He had assured Roll that he would stay at least that long in the valley. Could he ever agree to spend the rest of his life in the valley? Absolutely not was his first response to that question.

Jesus … a week ago I thought I needed questions answered. Now it's even worse. He leaned back on the seat and closed his eyes. At least he didn't have to decide right this minute.

Chapter 8

During the night of their first camp on the return trip it started to rain and everyone who was not in a tent was soon in a wagon or under one. The rain was slow but steady, a preamble to the coming fall season.

London had stretched his bedroll under Colleen's wagon and had only stirred slightly when some of the others crawled under next to him seeking a dry spot.

In the morning the reserve wood that was carried in the wagons to keep it dry was used to make the fires under the tent canopy. Breakfast was bacon, eggs, bread, jams and jellies.

When the wagons started out most of the drivers stood behind the seat and under the cover in an attempt to keep dry. The riders just toughed it out and rode in the rain.

No longer did the wagons travel in a straight line when it was possible to spread out. This way the wagons in the rear were not constantly forced to drive through the already churned up mud from the lead wagons. The first couple of days were slightly uphill but the loads had been well divided and six horse teams of Percherons had no trouble pulling the loads.

London dismounted and ran up behind Colleen's wagon. There were several horses tied to the tailgate and he looped his reins among the other fastenings. Trotting to reach the front, he leaped up and settled into the driver's seat taking the reins of the wagon's team from Colleen.

"Here, let me give you a break," he said.

Driving the big teams through the clinging soil was hard work and the leather reins were water soaked and heavy.

"Help yourself," she answered gratefully as she shrugged her shoulders and spent a couple of minutes stretching her arms and back.

Far ahead, overshadowing the rain clouds, a darker cloud had appeared.

"Red Fox," London called to one of his passengers, "what's that?"

The Indian peered ahead for a few seconds and said, "That is a cloud from the Rumbling Hills."

"That's not good," Colleen said over London's head. "It's been a year or more since the volcano acted up. Sometimes we get earthquakes and we've even seen it shoot lava into the air. Mother and I both feel it is dangerous but Father says it's nothing. I do know it scares me."

Word had spread quickly along the caravan. Ouseph, who was riding in the back of the wagon with Red Fox, called two of his men over who were still mounted on their horses. "Ride on ahead for a few miles," he said. "Make sure the trail is clear. We will be stopping for the night in the stand of trees where we sheltered on the way to town. Meet us there about sundown."

London watched as the two men left the train and galloped ahead. He turned to Red Fox and asked, "What's that all about?"

Red Fox leaned forward and spoke into London's ear. "When the mountain rumbles it is bad luck. That plus seeing the bears has made Chief Ouseph uneasy. He is sending riders ahead to check the trail."

"Not a bad idea," London said.

It was nearly dark when the wagons reached the stand of trees and the fresh water spring. First business was getting all the animals watered, grained and hobbled to graze near the camp. Ouseph, still disturbed by the bad signs, sent two more riders out, one to circle to the rear and the other to do the same thing ahead.

The evening meal was over when Red Fox shouted, "Riders coming in."

They were the two men that had been sent out earlier in the day to check the trail ahead. They rode to the cook fire and slid from their horses, one man falling when he did so. His left legging was soaked with blood from his waist to his ankle and he had lost his moccasin. Blood dripped from his bare foot.

Colleen hurried to the man and began her examination. Others crowded around the injured man and a rapid exchange in the Indian language ensued.

"What's going on?" London asked Red Fox.

"A party of Cheyenne attacked these two men," Red Fox answered. "They say it happened near the place where we saw the bears. The Cheyenne were laying in wait for the wagons and these men saw them and were trying to scout their camp when arrows came out of the dark and this man was hit."

"How many are there?" London asked.

"They say a large party, at least fifty or more," Red Fox said.

Ouseph walked over to London and said, "They saw the man we sent ahead and he has been warned. He will stay ahead and watch for anyone who might be following these men. Red Fox, you take two men with you and go ahead and aid this man. Make sure each man has a rifle."

"Is there anything I can do?" London asked Ouseph.

"Yes there is," Ouseph answered. "We must make a plan."

Colleen had finished treating the injured man and now she joined them saying, "He took an arrow high in the hip and he'll be sore for a few days but, thank goodness, it's not real serious."

Henri Merroux and Peter Digondo joined the group as Ouseph started to talk. "We're out manned but they're out gunned. If I know the Cheyenne, they would have waited in the trees on both sides of the trail and attacked us as we went up the valley. I'm sure their scouts know our strength."

Colleen looked at Ouseph and said, "So how do you think we should handle this?"

"Well, now that they know we're aware of their presence, they'll expect us to hold our camp. Instead of doing that I suggest we start up the valley at first light. We'll advance with the wagons two abreast with the riders between them. We'll stay to the extreme left along the tree line. The valley is more than a mile wide and they'll expect us to stay in the middle."

"When the Cheyenne attack," Ouseph went on, "they won't be able to come at us from both sides at the same time. I will send three men with our new rifles into the trees to get behind the Cheyenne so they will not be able to retreat to the cover of the trees once they attack. Here, let me show you what I mean."

Ouseph took a stick and began scratching lines in the dirt at their feet. Everyone could see the logic of his plan since their own force would be about equal to one-half the Cheyenne force. All of the best rifle shots would ride in the wagons nearest the tree line and when the charge was broken the riders would come around from both sides, forcing the attacking force back to the trees and the three rifles awaiting them.

The wagon would then form a circle and await the charge that was sure to come from across the valley. With the secured timberline at their back the mounted members would engage the survivors of the first attack and remain in reserve against the second attack.

At the first opportunity after the Cheyenne had committed all of their force, Star would break away and ride for the settlement and reinforcements. Using her Appaloosa no one should come close to catching her.

Ouseph quit drawing in the dirt and looked around. Everyone in the camp was looking at his drawings and listening to his instructions.

"Does anyone have anything they want to add?" Ouseph asked.

London spoke up and said, "As soon as the attack starts, pull the covers off the wagons so the rifles will have a full field of fire." Then London unbuckled his gun belt and handed it to Star. "Here, wear this in case one of the Cheyenne get to close."

"I hope I don't have to shoot any good looking ones," Star said as she buckled the belt around her waist.

"You won't think they're good looking if they catch you," Colleen said.

"Is there anything else anyone wants to bring up?" Ouseph said effectively cutting off the women's small talk.

Henri spoke. "The women should drive as many of the wagons as possible so we can have more men in the mounted party. The fighting will probably be the fiercest among the riders."

"Very well," Ouseph said. "Now let's get down to the specifics of who will be doing what."

The planning went on for two more hours and the travelers watched the rain clouds blow away and the stars come out promising clear weather for the day of the battle.

Just before sunrise the man who had been sent to the rear was summoned to camp and told of the situation and the plan for the battle. He exchanged for a fresh horse and joined the mounted unit between the double file of the six wagons. As soon as they started up the valley the front guard was gathered in and remounted so that now their forces were at full strength.

Three men with the small rifles had left much earlier on foot to make their way through the trees and take up a position of surprise at the enemy's rear. The wagons entered the valley in the center but immediately veered towards the tree line on the left and the plan started to develop.

The wagons were pulling sideways to the slope in the ground, holding down the speed of the caravan and making the attackers wait, something Ouseph believed would be to their advantage.

Up ahead as far as the eye could see the valley was pristine with the sun breaking golden on the wet and waving grassland. The party could see no living thing ahead of them.

Colleen was driving the lead wagon closest to the trees and London was riding at her side. All morning he had been completely unnerved by the situation. It was the danger to Colleen and to a lesser degree the others with the wagons that unsettled him. For years he had accepted the fact that he should have been killed a dozen times or more but he had always survived. He had accepted that he was a walking dead man and his life had been ever so much simpler without any fear.

London knew that every battle was unpredictable and allowing Ouseph to take all their lives into his hands was not what he truly wanted to do but he had decided that morning to accept the situation and just do his best to protect Colleen.

They were less than a hundred yards from the tree line when the first wave of attackers came charging at them. They were wearing paint on their bodies and were adorned with feathers in their hair and clothing. The small horses they were riding were mostly short legged and black and white in color, clearly no match for the powerful Appaloosas. The Cheyenne made no sound until the first shots were fired from the wagons and then they screamed and chanted as they charged.

The defenders in the wagons had pulled off the canvas tops and their first salvo dropped at least half a dozen men and horses. London stepped off his horse and tied his reins to the wagon wheel. Standing calmly he fired four shots, each slow and well aimed killing four of the onrushing Indians.

With their forces cut nearly in half in the first minute, the Cheyenne braves paused. At this point Ouseph's cavalry came around both ends of the wagons and had their enemy in a terrible crossfire.

The Cheyenne tried backing to the tree line but were greeted with a popping sound as the snipers in the trees opened fire. The slaughter was grim and great.

As soon as this issue was clearly decided all of the settlers and the Nez Perce warriors who were armed with rifles rushed back to the wagons to meet the second charge that was coming from across the valley. The remaining Nez Perce that were armed with bows and lances finished off the attackers from the first wave.

When the second charge was within fifty yards, all of the rifles opened fire. Men and horses fell like water over a dam, decimated by the concentrated fire of the defenders. The Cheyenne fell back out of rifle range and attempted to regroup. It was then that Star broke from the wagons and started up the valley at about three-quarter speed. She was a quarter mile gone before she was noticed and one Cheyenne started in pursuit.

Everyone in the wagon train watched her ride and it was immediately apparent that her pursuer had no chance of catching her unless her horse fell. Within five minutes the man who was chasing gave up and stopped his horse. A loud cheer went up from the wagons as Star disappeared over a rise.

Now the Cheyenne were in a quandary. Only four men had joined them from the first attacking group and they were down to less than half strength. Moreover with a rider escaping they knew help would be forthcoming. The Cheyenne could not believe that in such a short time they could be so humiliated.

It was then that London, Ouseph, and Red Fox rode out from the wagons and stopped at a point half way between the two groups.

The Cheyenne leader urged his horse forward and as the distance closed he saw a white man on a tall horse, a young Indian man and a third figure which caused him to stop and stare. His eyes opened wide as he recognized Chief Ouseph, the mighty leader of the Nez Perce. His posture sagged visibly as he nudged his pony forward.

Ouseph spoke first and said, "You may come and tend your wounded and carry off your dead. The battle is over. It would be best if you do not come again to our land unless it is in peace. If we again fight I tell you that none will remain to carry the dead back to your burial ground. I, Ouseph, have spoken."

The three turned their horses and rode back to the wagons, Red Fox repeating to London in English what Ouseph had told the Cheyenne.

The wagons held their position for just a short time before a half dozen of the Cheyenne came slowly to the site of the battle and began administering to their injured.

Colleen snapped her reins and the wagons began moving out leaving a rear guard of several Nez Perce with rifles in case of treachery by their enemies. London jumped from his horse onto the wagon seat next to Colleen and tossed his reins to Red Fox.

London looked deep into Colleen's eyes and studied her intently and said, "Are you okay?"

She sighed and nodded her head saying, "Yes, I'm fine. This is just the first time I ever shot anyone. I know of one man I killed and two others that I shot off their horses. I know … I know that …" And she leaned forward resting her head on her knees and began to sob uncontrollably.

London took the reins from her hands and put his arm across her shoulders attempting to comfort her. They rode that way for no more than a few minutes when Henri came riding up beside the wagon.

"Colleen," Henri called, "we need you back in the third wagon. One man is dead and four others are injured. Can you come?"

Colleen sat up and shook her head violently from side to side for a few seconds. "Of course," she said motioning Henri to ride closer. She grabbed her doctor's kit from the front floor of the wagon and jumped lithely over behind Henri and held on with one hand as he spun his horse to take her to her patients.

London looked back and saw her climb into one of the middle wagons. Further back he saw the rear guard spread out between them and the Cheyenne.

Red Fox came crawling through the wagon and settled on the seat beside London. "The horses are fastened on the back," he said.

As soon as his passenger looked comfortable London turned to him and asked, "You said you've known Colleen for a long time. What was she like growing up?"

"When we were children," Red Fox answered, "she was a … how do you say … a tom-boy. She would ride and hunt with the other young men and women of our people. She never searched for a husband like so many of the young women do. She was always interested in the medicine of our Shaman and she studied much in the books of her father."

"How do your people feel about her being a doctor?" London asked.

"They think it is good but when she left for her training many were afraid she would not return. Now she sometimes speaks as if she misses the excitement of other places."

Ah, London thought at once, maybe Colleen is not tied as tightly to this place as Roll believes. If persuasion becomes a factor this last bit of information could be real important.

"I would think," London said, "that after this morning she would have had enough excitement to last a lifetime. After the business of the old man last week and the battle today I'm beginning to think that this is a dangerous place to live."

"No," Red Fox said. "These were very unusual. Generally it's pretty peaceful and quiet around here."

London looked over at Red Fox and scrunched up his face as he said, "Okay, if you say so," but his disbelief was apparent.

"I wish to say something else," Red Fox said. "Again you fought bravely and I want to say that you have become a good friend in the short time you have been here."

"Thank you for saying so," London answered.

Then Red Fox added an afterthought that was to puzzle London for many days.

"I also hope that you would never become an enemy to anyone in the settlement or of my people," the Indian said.

The wagons were now traveling up the middle of the valley with only two men as a rear guard. It was late in the afternoon when the relief party from the settlement was seen in the distance. As they got close, London and Colleen who were once again in the lead wagon could see that Roll, Helen and Star were leading the way and about thirty riders leading a dozen extra horses were close behind. The wagons came to a stop and waited.

Helen and Roll stopped at the first wagon and Helen asked Colleen, "Are you all right ... and Josh, he's not hurt is he?"

The others who were in the rescue party scattered among the wagons checking on friends and family as Colleen answered, "We're both just fine. One of the Nez Perce was killed in the battle and another died this afternoon from his wounds. Another Indian and two of our people were injured but not seriously."

Helen swung from her horse onto the seat beside her daughter and hugged her with relief. "Tell me what happened," Helen said.

Roll stepped from his horse and waited as London jumped down from the wagon seat and joined him.

"Are you hurt?" Roll asked London.

"No, I'm fine," London answered as Star rode up beside them.

She leaned down and handed London his gun belt and said, "Thank goodness I didn't need this but there is something I need now."

"What's that?" London asked.

"If there is room in the back of that wagon, I'm going to crawl back there and go to sleep," she said.

"Then here you go," London said taking one of her arms while Roll took the other one. After a big lift Star found herself on the wagon seat beside Helen and Colleen. After a smile all around Star flopped over backward from the seat and landed on a stack of grain sacks.

"We brought extra horses," Roll said, "and two men are following with eight more Percherons to help in case any were hurt in the battle."

"You can check with Henri," London answered, "but I think the horses are fine. We were planning on stopping early since it has been a pretty long day and that will be a good time to check all the animals."

"Sounds just right," Roll said. "Now I'm going to ride back and find Ouseph. I'll see you in a little bit."

London looked up at Colleen and Helen on the front seat of the wagon. Colleen was talking a mile a minute and Helen was mostly just nodding and listening to the story of the battle.

London walked to the rear of the wagon where his horse was tied and swung into the saddle, alone with his thoughts for a few minutes. How many more had he killed this day, six, ten ... maybe a dozen. He kicked his horse into motion and cantered ahead of the wagons until he was a couple of miles ahead.

Sure he was alone, London stopped his horse and sat in the saddle shaking all over. Tears ran down his cheeks. What the hell is wrong with me, he thought. I've never acted this way before. Battles, danger or gunplay never made me nervous. Now, all of a sudden, just being with Colleen and the others is affecting me in ways I never imagined.

London shook his head violently from side to side to try and clear his thoughts. Get a hold of yourself, he thought. Get your mind straight. He stepped down from his horse and sat down on the ground where he stayed until the wagons were starting to close on him. He climbed back into the saddle and rejoined the train, pretty much back to normal.

When they stopped for the day, Ouseph and Roll came riding in with the others in the rear guard and Ouseph called out four men who had been resting in the wagons and sent them to the rear to keep watch.

After checking the animals, a meal was the next order of business and soon everyone was gathered around the cooking fires reliving the events of the day.

"Friend Roll," Ouseph was saying, "we have seen many bad omens in the last few days and now two of my people are dead."

"Yes, but London tells me the battle was swiftly won by your good plan," Roll answered.

"But brave men died, some of ours and a great many of theirs and there is no glory in death," Ouseph said.

"True words," Roll replied, "but your plan allowed my son and daughter to escape danger. If we had lost another child so quickly it would have been very unsettling. Helen and I again thank you for what you did."

"Maybe so," Ouseph said, "but if you had seen how your friend London could fight then perhaps our help would not have been needed. It is possible he could handle fifty Cheyenne by himself."

London and the others laughed at the Chief's joke but the participants of the battle who had seen London in his killing mode had been awestruck by his efficiency.

The spare draft horses arrived and now Roll and Ouseph were going to send two of them to carry the Indians who had died in the battle back to their own main camp for proper burial. Two spare wagon wheels were used to fashion a cart for transport. It would take five days to reach the main Nez Perce camp with the wagons slowing down the transporting party. They were planning to leave the first thing in the morning.

With everyone now fed, the people divided up into mostly family groups. Since the rain there had been a slight edge to the breeze so the cooking fires had not been allowed to go out. In the glow Roll, Helen, Josh, Colleen and London sat and talked.

"We saw more smoke from the volcano," Colleen said. "How much activity was there?"

"More than enough," Helen said. "We had earth tremors and a crack opened up in the ground about half a mile back from the Escarpment.'

"What sort of crack?" Josh asked.

Roll explained by saying, "It appears that a layer of rock starts at the edge of the Escarpment and dips down and curves back up where the crack occurred. In between the rock is covered with topsoil to what depth I have no idea. It's possible the rock shifted due to the volcanic activity and that caused the crack."

"We told you that mountain was dangerous," Colleen said.

"I didn't say it was dangerous," Roll answered. "We all know from the geology books that the earth's crust is unstable. The shifting of the ground is perfectly normal in the mountains."

"How big a crack is it?" Josh asked.

"Not big," Helen said, "but it will need to be filled with dirt so the animals or kids don't break a leg. About a foot wide and twice as deep would be my guess."

London had been listening intently asked, "Has anything like this ever happened before?"

"We have had several eruptions and tremors since we've been here but we never had a crack open up in the area of the settlement," Helen said.

"Enough of this," Roll said. "We have been doing something else while you've been gone. What Colleen said about London's idea for heat has kept me busy. Helen designed a system and I have been working on a model that I'm going to expand and use for heat in at least one home this winter. Since London will be needing a home of his own we are going to design it with steam heating in the plan."

"Wait a minute," London said. "Do I really need a whole house of my own? Maybe I could just stay in the visitors cabin until I decide what I'm going to do in the spring."

"Are you saying you might be leaving?" Josh asked in disbelief, the concept of going away foreign to his thinking.

"I don't know," London answered. "I haven't decided what I am going to do."

"You've seen what the outside world is like," Roll said. "What could possibly be better than our life here?"

"Well, I've never seen San Francisco and that is where I was planning to go when I left here," London said.

"What's in San Francisco?" Helen asked.

"Maybe nothing," London replied, "But I have a stake of money in the bank in Denver. I had thought about opening a gambling house somewhere."

"But nobody can leave," Josh said. "That's the rule."

Roll responded to Josh's statement much too quickly as he said, "We have until spring to decide this. For now, why don't we just turn in for the night. It's been a long hard day for everyone."

The next day on the trail London and Roll were riding ahead of the wagons and talking.

"You really have caught us at a bad time," Roll was saying. "We generally don't have this much excitement in a year."

"I believe you," London replied, "but these last few days have been far from boring."

"Yes, but you remember that when you first came I told you that this was a unique community with unique rules," Roll said.

"So you said," London answered, "but in regards to the conversation last evening, YOU remember that I didn't promise to stay here past next spring. If I decide to leave, I WILL leave."

London spoke this last statement with great emphasis on the word 'will' and Roll's head snapped at the resolve he heard in London's voice.

Roll took a deep breath and answered slowly, saying, "That's all in time to come. For now let's just make the best of life and let things come as they may."

London thought he heard some reconciliation in Roll's voice. Maybe his friend was not going to be quite as adamant as he feared. Okay, he thought, we'll wait and see.

The sound of hoof beats caused them to look around and see Colleen riding up to join them. "What are you two gabbing about, blood and battles?" she asked.

"Not at all," Roll said, "just the weather and the volcano. I have decided to give the rumbling mountain a name. From now on it will be called Mount Helen after your mother."

"Oh dear!!" Colleen said. "I don't think she's going to take kindly to that."

"Oh, I think your mother has a sense of humor," Roll said, "and besides every landmark should have a name."

They were all chuckling when London added, "You should be the one to tell her, Roll. That's one dangerous job I refuse to accept."

"Just to show you my courage, I'll go and tell her right now," Roll said as he spun his horse around and headed for the lead wagon where Helen was driving.

Ironically Colleen brought up the same topic that London and Roll had been discussing when she said, "You know Father really wants you to stay with us and I would like for you to stay also."

"You've only known me for a few days," London said. "How can you be so sure?"

"When I was away from the valley I saw that most men treat women as inferiors. Here we are all equal, even among the Indians. It

90

was awful back east to be a second class person because I'm a woman. You don't make me feel that way."

Colleen continued to talk. "Oh, I saw how you tried to stay close during the battle and tried to protect me but that's not the same. You let me do my job and have my say and most often you behave towards me like an equal. I appreciate that."

"You're intelligent, capable and beautiful," London said. "How could anyone see you any other way?"

"My oh my, those are kind words from a man who has lived on the Mississippi river boats and seen so much," she answered.

London stopped his horse and looked at her closely as he said, "Those are true words as our Indian friends would say."

Colleen stared back, slightly flustered and, to cover her confusion raised her canteen and said, "I'll drink to that." She took a deep swallow and then passed the water on to London.

"Me too," he said.

Roll and Helen were watching the couple ahead. He had just finished telling her of the name he had given the volcano and she had reluctantly gone along. Now as they saw London and Colleen share a drink from the canteen, Helen was saying, "There are so few eligible men and to have someone as fitting as London show up it's almost miraculous."

"Yes, he is a good man," Roll said, "but Colleen will have the final say in those matters, I'm sure."

"She generally does," Helen agreed.

Then Roll made a statement that gave Helen a feeling of dread deep inside. "However it works out between those two, I have decided that London will have to stay here at the settlement. If I were to allow him to leave it would set a precedent that would make maintaining order here impossible and that is unacceptable to me."

"But if he would insist on leaving what could you do?" Helen asked.

"First I would try to talk him out of it and if that failed I would just have to stop him," Roll answered.

Helen studied the face of the man she loved and admired and said nothing. She prayed that such a confrontation would never take place. Two men, both solid and set in their ways … it could only end one way.

Chapter 9

London sat at the large table in Roll's study room in the main house. London had been feeling guilty about not having a job of his own at the settlement so Roll had delegated him a duty that Roll himself had been putting off for some time. There were two stacks of writing paper in front of him, one stack new paper and the other covered with his first draft of his story about the settlement here at the Escarpment. He had been working all through the early part of the morning as had been his custom for the last month. Soon he would leave the study and walk to where the new house was being built.

It would be a grand house, two stories high with a full basement and a porch around three sides. With four bedrooms and two bathrooms it seemed more luxurious than practical but Roll had said it was to be to test the use of steam heat and the house was just an elaborate experiment.

When they had returned from the last trip to town London had found that the basement was well started. The dirt had been loaded into wagons and was being used to fill the crack caused by the earth tremor. The volcano had continued to belch forth smoke and fumes but there had been no more seismic activity.

The writing had been progressing nicely and London was spending time with each resident getting their personal stories and learning how they ended up at the Escarpment. On three different occasions the name of Diego Vargas had come up. He had been an early settler who had set up the farming program for the community. When London had asked to interview Vargas he found that the man was no longer in the camp and everyone was vague about his history and his present whereabouts.

"Talk to Roll," everyone had told him when he tried to pin him down. Even Colleen said she did not know the whole story and had told him that either her Father or Mother would have to give him the details.

London felt now was the time to add this chapter to his story and he set out to find Roll with the question of Diego Vargas firmly in his mind.

London headed for where the new house was being built knowing that was where he would find Roll. All the framing was done and the trenches that held the pipes and tiles from their own kiln and smelter were in place to bring in the gas and water and carry off the bathroom and kitchen wastes.

In the center of one inside wall was a stone chimney serving the dual purpose of carrying off the smoke from the main room fireplace and the kitchen cooking stove heat. Inside all the walls were redwood and cedar with every board hand polished until it glowed.

At Colleen's insistence the small fixtures around the walls for the gas-lights were once again being made from gold. A steel alloy was being used for the huge chandeliers however.

London walked up the stone steps and through the front door. He didn't see anyone and he called out, "Is anybody here?"

"Up here," came a voice from the second floor.

London ran up the stairs two at a time and found Sean McNamara and Roll working in the bedroom closets. They were building shelves of the same wood as the closet walls using the finest hand polished cedar.

"Roll, this is sure some house," London said. "If the president of the world ever came to visit you'll definitely have a place for him to stay."

"Every house we build seems to be better than the one before," Sean said. "Of course our sawmill and wood working shops are turning out better products than when we first started."

"That is something I'm writing into the story of the settlement,"

London said. "I'm trying to credit each of the residents with the skill and knowledge they have brought to the Escarpment."

"That's a good idea," Roll said, "and how is it going?"

"I do have a couple of small problems," London said. "The first is why do you want a written history of the settlement if you intend to keep it secret and private."

Roll answered with a wry grin as he said, "I know that in the years to come all this country will be settled and I would like the people who eventually settle here to know of how it all began."

"Okay," London answered, "and now for the second problem and it's with a man called Diego Vargas."

"I knew sooner or later you would come to him," Roll said

"Everyone who has mentioned his name has been reluctant to talk about the man. They all say I should talk to you about that story," London said.

"Well I guess I should be the one to tell you about what happened with Diego," Roll replied. "After lunch we'll sit down in the study room and I'll tell you the story from start to finish. It's something we are not real proud of."

"That'll suit me just fine," London said, his curiosity on one point finally going to be satisfied.

Diego Vargas had been a hired hand at a great hacienda in Spain. He was intelligent and industrious and familiar with all the aspects of the operation of the large ranch. He was especially adept at farming and his grapes were considered the finest in the region. He was also good with horses and when not in the vineyards, he was in the stables.

It was here that he met Conseulo who was the daughter of the owner of the huge ranch. He would prepare her horse for her to go riding and take it from her when she finished. Being young and foolish, they fell in love.

Both knew well that Conseulo's father would not only

disapprove of their relationship but would put a stop to it by any means necessary. But the family of Conseulo was very wealthy and she had inherited a great deal of valuable jewelry. Diego and Conseulo decided to take the jewels and run far away to Portugal where they would buy a small ranch and live out their days.

This they did and the happiness they shared lasted for several years until Conseulo's family tracked them down with the intent of killing Diego for robbing them of their daughter.

Diego, learning of the plot, quickly sold their fine farm and once again they fled, this time to America. They now had three children and they settled in South Carolina where once again Diego started farming, this time raising cotton and tobacco. He was successful in a modest form but he would not buy or use slaves on his land. The blacks who did come to his place were mostly runaways who he allowed to stay and work as free men. Occasionally this led to minor altercations with some of the local authorities but he was lucky and never got into any real trouble.

When the spotted sickness called measles swept through that area of the United States children died by the thousands. All three of the Vargas children died within the same week. Conseulo could no longer stand to live where her children had been taken from her so this time they headed west.

After months of travel, they ended up at the Escarpment as others had done and decided to leave the wagon train they were with and stay on as residents.

Diego's farming skills were incredible and within two years he had cleared land and grown an assortment of crops that soon graced the tables of the entire settlement.

Conseulo also found her place in the community. Still grieving the loss of her children she established a nursery in her home and cared for all the children whose parents had other duties.

Diego and Conseulo were loved by all and they were happy in their new home.

One winter, after a cold and rainy spell, Conseulo developed a cough that would not leave her. During the summer when the weather was warm and dry the cough was not as bad but still did not seem to get any better. That next winter she died, drowned by the fluid that was in her lungs.

Over the years Diego had grown grapes and made wine that was stored in a cool cave near the snow line. Barrels had been taken up more often than they were brought back down. With the death of Conseulo, Diego spent more and more time at the cave chasing away the demons of his life with drunkenness. He was a broken man and who could really blame him.

Late at night during the summer Diego took all of the jewelry that was left from Conseulo's fortune and carried it to the camp's gold cache. Leaving the jewelry in its place Diego took a dozen one pound bars of pure gold and left the camp with supplies for the trail and two horses.

The next day Roll and Miguel Sanchez set out to bring him back.

Diego gave them quite a run and they didn't catch up with him until after he had reached Denver. Luckily Diego had some money of his own and when they found him he still had all the gold he had taken from the settlement. Roll and Miguel brought him home and tried to help him recover from his losses.

Diego would not, or could not, respond. It was then that Roll Jacobs took a stand and told Diego that the only way he would be allowed to leave the settlement was over the Escarpment.

Cold? Cruel? Maybe so. Roll felt it was the only way to maintain the integrity of the camp. At that time only Helen, Roll and Miguel knew of the ultimatum that had been given to Diego Vargas.

A week later in the early morning Diego went to see Henri Merroux at the corral and got a horse. As he rode away from the barn he shouted back, "Tell Roll I'm leaving as he suggested."

Neither Diego Vargas nor the horse was ever seen again.

"That's some story," London said looking across the table at Roll and Helen.

"Do you think we did wrong?" Helen asked.

"How can I be a judge?" London replied. "Under similar circumstances I might have done the same thing."

"We've agonized over the decision for many years," Roll said. "At the time it seemed like the right thing to do but now ... who knows ... maybe we would handle it differently."

"How much of the story do the other settlers know?" London asked.

"Most all of it, I'm sure," Helen said.

"How do you want me to write it up in the history of the settlement?" London asked.

"However you think is best," Roll answered. "If you wish you can put it down just the way we told it to you."

"Isn't that a lot to ask your children to understand when they read this story," London said indicating the stacks of paper on the table.

"That's not the way we look at it," Roll explained. "We're not asking for approval, we're just telling what was done. Now it's over and nothing anyone can say or do will change what happened."

"I guess it's really not much different from what happened to the old prospector," London said quietly.

Chapter 10

It was a bright Indian summer day and London and Colleen sat near the edge of the Escarpment. Colleen had just finished reading the story of Diego Vargas.

"What do you think," London asked her

"Most of the story I already knew," she said. "It was only the end that that I didn't know about. I'm sure Father thought he was doing the right thing."

"I'm sure he believed that at the time," London replied, "but strangers are going to continue to come here and sooner or later someone else is going to want to leave."

"Have you asked Father about this?" she said.

"Not yet," London answered. "He and your mother just told me the story yesterday and I wrote it last night. I really haven't had enough time to think about it yet."

"Has anyone else read what you've written?" she asked.

"No. I wanted to get your opinion first." London said.

"Personally, I understand why he handled the situation in the way he did. Diego Vargas had become a drunkard and could no longer be trusted to keep the secrets of the settlement," she said.

"You can't hide a community of this size forever," London answered somewhat impatiently. Although he had expected Colleen to defend her father's actions, he was having some trouble accepting Roll's pitiless behavior.

"I'm sure Father has many good reasons for acting the way he does," Colleen said. "You know that his life away from here has been very unpleasant."

"You were away for a time," London answered, "and you know that there is good and bad everywhere. You can't hide forever from the rest of the world."

As if to punctuate London's statement Colleen said, "Look."

A young boy was busy pulling the red flag up the flagpole.

Colleen and London saw a young woman with a rifle across her saddle heading up the valley at a gallop to meet the incoming guard. They walked towards the house under construction where they expected to find Roll and he was just stepping off the porch when they arrived.

"Come with me," Roll said to them and headed at a brisk walk towards his house and ducked in the front door reemerging within seconds with a telescope in his hand.

Henri came galloping around the corner, jerked his horse to a sliding stop and shouted, "The barn is secure and now I'm headed for the shops and the power plant to shut them down," and rode off at full speed.

"Can you see anything?" Colleen asked her father as he turned the telescope in the direction of the incoming visitors.

Roll just shook his head and they all waited.

When the riders did come into view Roll said, "Guard and two men, both big and leading a pack horse. I don't recognize them. Here London, you take a look."

London looked for several seconds and said, "Yeah, I know them. They were in town when we were there. Buffalo hunters, I think."

Colleen took the glass, got a good look and said, "Yep, that's them. They gave us some trouble in the store. A couple of real animals."

London walked into the house and came back out wearing his six-gun.

Roll raised his voice and hollered into the house. "Helen, fix some sandwiches and coffee and bring it to the barn. We'll meet these two pilgrims there."

Colleen went inside to help her mother as Roll and London

started walking towards the barn.

Sean McNamara had joined London and Roll at the barn when Miguel Sanchez brought the two men into the settlement. London stood back leaning against a corral post as Roll greeted the men.

"Afternoon gentlemen," Roll said, "what can I do for you?"

"Howdy," the taller man said. "My name's Ed Huggins and this here's Lou Smith. We're up here lookin' for a prospector that headed this way about a month or so ago and ain't never come back to town. His brother's kinda' worried and gave us'n twenty dollars and supplies to come up and see if we could find him."

"What makes you think he came here?" Roll asked.

"Oh, he was here afores' and this place is about all he ever talked about ever since," Huggins said.

"Yeah, he was here way back," Roll said, "and we fed him and he left."

It was just about then that Ed Huggins recognized London and said, "Howdy there, Mister London. Nice seein' you again."

"Yeah, Mister London," the second man said. "No hard feelings' about that little thing in town. We was just drinking an' … aw hell … you know how it is."

"I surely do," London answered with a slow nod of the head.

"Anyway," Ed want on, "we was just wondering' if he might of come back here? He said he was gonna' do some digging' in the hills up to the north."

"That's Nez Perce land," Roll said. "If he started digging up there they would be sure to run him off."

"I hear'd he was a stubborn old man," Lou Smith said. "Supposing he wouldn't go?"

"If the Nez Perce say to leave, you'll leave," Roll said.

"How do you mean?" Ed Huggins asked. "Do you think they might'a kilt him?"

"No, I wouldn't think so," Roll answered. "They'd just make sure he moved on."

It was at this point in the conversation that Colleen and Henri rode up from the houses and joined the group.

"Hey," Lou Smith said, "That's the guy that kicked the shit out'ta you in the store that day, Ed. And that gal there is the one that was with him."

"Shaddup Lou," Ed Huggins said. "Again I wanta' say we're sorry for the way we acted that day. Like we said, we was drinking pretty heavy," and he looked towards Colleen and pulled the front of his greasy hat and added, "Sorry missy."

"Yes'am, me too," Lou Smith said with a broken toothed grin and a smile.

Colleen dismounted and set a basket containing half a dozen sandwiches and a pot of coffee on the edge of the watering trough. "Here's some food and coffee," was all she said.

Both men stepped from their horses and began pawing through the basket tearing off chunks of sandwich and stuffing them into their mouths and down their throats with scarcely a chew along the way. Although there were cups in the basket they drank the coffee straight from the pot, passing it back and forth.

In five minutes the food was gone and London said, "You boys want to count your fingers and make sure you didn't swallow one by mistake?"

The joke went right over their heads as they spread their fingers out in front of them and Lou Smith said, "Aw hell, Mister London, I can't count."

Colleen grabbed up the empty basket and vaulted onto her horse, heading towards the houses but before she got out of hearing range her whoops of laughter caused Lou and Ed to look after her curiously and frown, wondering what they had missed.

Ed Huggins looked over at the residents and asked, "Is one of you fellas Roll Jacobs?"

"I am," Roll answered.

"The folks in town said you had a really big spread up here," Ed said. "They told us if we was gonna' try to talk to the Indians we should see you first to find out what's what."

"The best advice I can give you," Roll answered, "is to keep moving when you're in Indian country. They don't seem to mind if you pass through but if you start shooting buffalo or hunting for gold they could get pretty mad."

"You suppose they might have seen the old man and would they tell us if they did?" Ed asked.

"More than likely they'd tell you what they know," Roll said.

As they had been talking both Ed and Lou had been admiring the barn adjacent to the corral and it was Lou that asked, "Mister Jacobs, how would it be if me and Ed was to stay in your big ole' barn tonight? We could just stick our horses in this here corral an' sleep in there on the hay. We wouldn't be no bother to nobody."

"Sorry boys," Roll said. "By dark you're gonna' be past the tree line and moving along at a steady pace."

"Well now that ain't very friendly," Ed Huggins said.

"Boys, I'd say we been right accommodating," Roll said curtly, his hands on his hip and his eyes squinted. "We answered all your questions, fed you and we're going to give you plenty of fresh water for your horses and canteens. And to make sure you don't get lost I'm gonna' ask London here to ride with you so it'll be easy to keep going in a straight line."

The two large and dirty men looked over at London leaning against the rail around the corral and saw him smile at them in a way that they didn't think was exactly friendly and they immediately understood what Roll meant.

"Right as rain, Mister Jacobs," Ed Huggins said as Lou Smith nodded rapidly in agreement and they renewed their water supply as London saddled his horse and slid the Henry rifle Miguel had been carrying into the scabbard on his horse.

"In case of a grizzly," London said dryly and they were on their way.

With the wind at their back London rode about a length behind Ed and Lou. He didn't think the two men would give him any trouble but he was concerned that they might harass the woman who was now acting as guard.

"Why wouldn't Jacobs let us stay in his barn?" Ed asked back over his shoulder.

"I guess because it's his place and he can do pretty much as he likes," London answered.

"Yep, I suppose," Ed said, "but he let you stay. Why was that?"

"We're old friends from the war and he invited me to come and visit for a while," London replied.

"Did you two fight together in the war?" Lou Smith asked.

"No," London said. "We were both in Andersonville when the war ended."

"What's that?" Ed asked.

"Andersonville was in Georgia," London said. "It was a Rebel prison for captured Union soldiers."

"You're a jail bird, huh?" Lou said.

"I guess you could say that," London answered with a wry smile.

"I been in jail," Lou Smith said with a grin and certain amount of pride.

"That's nice," London replied

"Shaddup Lou. He don't want to listen to your gab," Ed said and went on saying, "Mister London do you suppose you could point us on the way to where we could find the Injuns?"

"I'm sure if you keep heading north you should find them soon enough or they'll find you," London said. "But I gotta' tell you that a while back a party of Cheyenne were raiding in this area and if you should happen to run into them you would be in a lot of trouble."

"I didn't think the Cheyenne came this far north," Ed said.

"They was here," London answered, "and the Nez Perce killed about half the party and sent the rest back home with orders to stay there." London did not see any sense in mentioning the settlers' part in the battle.

"You mean the Nez Perce whipped up on the Cheyenne? That surely is a surprise to me," Ed said.

"They just don't take to kindly to anyone coming onto their land uninvited," London answered. "If I was you two I'd mind my manners with them."

Ahead at the tree line was a rider on a horse. "Hey—Hey," Ed Huggins said, "that's the woman we seen riding up the valley on our way in."

"Yeah, it is," London said. "This is where I stop. You boys just keep on riding for at least two more hours before you stop for the night and there won't be no problems."

"Sure enough, Mister London," Ed said, "an' I don't blame you one bit for wanting to stop here with this gal."

"Just keep riding," London said abruptly and he steered his horse to where the woman sat on her horse.

The woman spoke first saying, "I'm Delores Sanchez, Miguel's wife."

London had seen her around the settlement but had never talked with her. He was impressed with her good looks and self control at being out here all alone.

"I'm very pleased to meet you," London said. "Aren't you a little nervous being up here all by yourself?"

"Not really," she said. "My husband taught me to shoot and up until just recently I was the best rifle shot in the settlement. Now my husband tells me that I'm second best since he saw you shoot. The only thing that bothers me about being up here is the occasional grizzly."

London really enjoyed listening to the woman talk, her English strongly flavored with a Spanish accent.

"Well that pair that just left could be more dangerous than a bear," London said, "specially if they got the upper hand with a woman."

"In this valley we all do our jobs," Delores said.

"So I've seen," London answered. "Then I guess you don't think it's necessary for me to wait around to make sure those two don't come back?"

"No. If they come back, I'll handle it and then light the fire for the night time signal," she said.

"Good enough, Delores," London said. "I'll be seeing you back at the settlement," and he headed back down the valley, cantering his horse.

A mile or so before he reached the settlement London saw a rider ahead. It was Colleen and her gray horse looked like a ghost in the moonlight.

"Howdy there lady," he said. "What's a nice girl like you doing in a place like this?"

"Just waiting for you," she answered. "Did your escort go okay?"

"Yep, except I was a little concerned about Delores Sanchez being up there all by herself," he said.

There was a slight edge of impatience to Colleen's voice when she said, "I thought you were getting over that attitude. Women are just as capable as men at most of the jobs around here. Except for the cleaning of stables we're all equal."

London laughed. "I take it you don't like to clean stables."

"Who does?" she answered.

They stepped down from their horses and started walking towards the settlement, not being in any hurry to get there. Their breaths were light clouds in front of their faces as they talked and frost was starting to settle on the grass, wetting their boots.

"Cold weather is not far away," she said. "The snow is not so bad here in the valley but the passes to the south will be blocked and the only place there is to go is the Chopunnish camp to the northeast. We go there at least once each winter just for a change of scenery."

"I haven't got tired of the scenery around here yet," London said. "I could still stand on the edge of the Escarpment every day. Somehow it seems different every time I look at it."

"Yes," she said, "I know what you mean."

"And something else," he said, "I like looking at you every day."

"Oh my," she said, "really."

"Every night I think about the night you kissed me at the door of my room. It was wonderful."

"Then maybe we ought to do it again," she said as she turned to him and held his body tight against her as she threw her arms around his neck and gave him a long, slow, wet kiss.

When they leaned away he said, "Lordy, if every time gets better I could stand a lot more of that."

"Privacy is a rare commodity in the settlement," she said. "In a couple of weeks your own house will be done and then we'll see even less of each other."

"Two weeks, you say," London answered. "In that case we better not waste much time," and this time he leaned over and kissed her.

Chapter 11

"Ya know, Ed" Lou Smith was saying, "maybe that London is not as bad as we think. What say we circle back and see what him and that little gal is doin'? Huh Ed, what'ta ya say?"

"You can go back if you want'a but if he sees you he'll kill ya for sure and certain." Ed answered.

"He sure don't seem that tough to me," Lou said.

"LISTEN HERE," Ed shouted, "You go back if you want'a but I'm keeping the supplies and grub with me 'cause an hour from now you ain't gonna' be needing none of it, you hear me!"

"Aw hell, Ed, I was just talkin'. You know I ain't gonna' go against you. Now how far we gonna' go afore we camp?" Lou asked.

"He said we was to go out of sight beyond the trees for two hours," Ed said. "I figure on going at least twice that far."

"Okay Ed, I was just thinking, that's all," Lou said.

"Your gonna' think your way straight into a grave," Ed answered. "Now you just shut your trap and let's keep riding for a while."

It was near midnight when Ed and Lou hung their canvas shelter from a tree branch and made camp. They hobbled their horses and built a small fire to fry bacon in a greasy skillet. They used their fingers to stuff it in their mouths and swallowed it without chewing. Lou boiled a pot of coffee and they drank half of it passing the pot back and forth as was their custom and saved the other half for morning. Five minutes after they stretched out on the ground the snores coming forth would have frightened off a grizzly.

For the next two days they headed steadily northeast in the foothills of the mountains. They could see smoke from the volcano to the northwest and used that as their reference point.

Although they were sure they were in the Nez Perce country they had not seen a single Indian. But the Indians had seen them.

Two men from Ouseph's camp were hunting elk and had been more or less following and watching the movements of Ed Huggins and Lou Smith for the last day and a half. As they neared the main Nez Perce camp one of the Indians rode on ahead and the other continued to watch the two men.

When the two buffalo hunters finally rode into the Nez Perce camp, everyone knew they were coming and nobody paid them any attention what so ever. Camp life went on as though the two searchers were invisible.

There were more than two hundred shelters that Ed and Lou could see as they sat on their horses looking around the camp. On one side was a huge split rail corral holding nearly a thousand horses with most of them being Appaloosas.

"Ya know, Ed," Lou Smith said, "This would be a hell of a good place to steal some horses."

Ed looked around at the bustling camp and the hundreds of Indians and shook his head as he said, "It's a wonder you've lived as long as you have."

"Hey, looka' there," Lou said as a child ran across in front of them. "That was a little white kid but he was dressed like an Injun."

"What do ya suppose that means?" Ed Huggins said.

"Must be a captive," Lou said. "These redskins must have stole him from a wagon train or something."

"Hey maybe if we don't find the old man we could rescue the kid and take him back an' get a reward," Ed said.

"Look over there," Lou said. "Two more white kids playin' with those little Injuns."

"Hey Ed," Lou said, "maybe we're onto something here."

As Lou and Ed had been talking an Indian man had walked over near their horses and stood looking at them. It was Red Fox and he listened intently to their conversation.

Ed Huggins noticed Red Fox and held up his hand, palm out and said, "How ... we friends ... you understand ... friends."

Red Fox folded his arms across his chest and with a perfectly straight face said, "Ugh."

"You know any of this Injun lingo, Lou?" Ed asked.

"Nope, I ain't heard them say anything yet," Lou answered. "What about you?"

"Me neither," Ed said.

"How ... Ugh ...," Red Fox said as he held up his hands mimicking Ed Huggins' gestures.

"How the hell are we gonna' talk to these dumb ass Injuns," Lou said.

"Ugh ... dumbassinjuns," Red Fox said in a deep monotone.

"Then how are we gonna' ask them if they seen the old man," Lou said. "How about tryin' to use sign language on them?"

"What would be the sign for white man, I wonder," Ed said.

"Point at yourself and say 'white man,'" Lou said.

"White man ... white man," Ed said pointing at his chest and rubbing his face.

"Ugly as a buffalo," Red Fox said in his own language.

"Hey, he understands. You see other white man?" Ed said pointing at his eye and then at Red Fox.

By this time several other Indians had gathered around and were stoically listening to the conversation.

"These are the two buffalo hunters we saw in town," Red Fox said in his own language to the people who had stopped to listen. "They are the ones who called Morning and Star 'dirty Injuns'."

"Ahhh," the crowd said as they nodded and stared at the two men.

"I think we're getting somewhere," Ed said. "The man we're looking for was riding a mule. You understand ... mule?" and he held his fingers up beside his ears pointing up and went, "Hee-Haw ... Hee-Haw."

None of the Indians even cracked a smile as Red Fox said, "That sure does seem appropriate for you fellas," still in his own language.

A young Indian boy stepped from the crowd that had gathered and spoke to Red Fox. "Are you going to let them know that most of us speak English?" he asked.

"Not just yet," Red Fox said. "Listening to them and watching their sign language is too much fun. I'm going to point off to the east and make them believe I understand their signs. That way they'll just move on and we'll be done with them."

Red Fox pointed at his cheek and then at Ed. He made the motion of riding a horse and pointed at the distant mountains.

"By golly Ed, I think you done it," Lou said. "I think he's saying that the old man went thataway."

"Yep, that's what I figure too," Ed said. "Now let's see if we can do some horse trading with these stupid Injuns."

Ed stepped from his horse and motioned for Red Fox to follow him. Leading his horse with one hand Ed headed for the corral holding the herd of Appaloosa horses. At the fence he handed the reins of his horse to Red Fox and indicated the horses in the corral and finally pointed at himself. "Me want trade," Ed said, "understand ... trade?"

"Ugh ... trade," Red Fox said.

"You're not really going to trade horses with these two, are you?" a man from the crowd asked.

"No," Red Fox answered, "but how would you like to see these two fat men try and put a saddle on one of our best stallions? As long as we're here to make sure the horse doesn't get hurt it should be a lot of fun."

"Hey, good idea," the man said, "but take your time making the deal. Everyone in camp would like to watch this," and he hurried off to spread the word.

Star and Morning had joined the crowd and were standing well back not wishing to be recognized but anxious for revenge for the insults they had suffered in town.

After a few minutes of negotiating and with the entire camp watching, Red Fox pointed to a horse in the corral and Ed nodded his head. Red Fox entered the corral and threw a rope around the neck of their most aggressive stallion. This horse was only used for stud and never for riding. Believing he was being taken to a mare the horse remained docile enough as he was tied to the fence.

Red Fox stepped away and Ed approached the horse carrying his saddle blanket and saddle. The horse only pranced and acted skittish when the blanket was tossed on his back. Then Ed topped off the blanket with the saddle and all hell broke loose.

Red Fox had tied the halter rope securely to the top of the rail fence and the horse immediately pulled the rail loose and it began swinging around as the horse went berserk. Ed grabbed the rail as a reflex action in self-defense and hung on for dear life. Up and down, back and forth, around and around went Ed Huggins.

The Indians were hysterical with laughter as the man tried to escape from the ferocious animal.

Meanwhile Lou Smith, who had unsaddled his horse in preparation for the trade was putting his saddle back on his own mount.

Ed finally got loose from the wild Appaloosa and dove under the fence escaping by inches with his life. The horse, now that Ed was gone took out his vengeance on Ed's saddle, pounding it into mush with his powerful hoofs.

Red Fox and another man jumped into the corral and gentled the horse at the same time motioning for Ed to come and get his blanket and badly battered saddle.

Ed ducked into the corral, grabbed his equipment and just as quickly ducked back out. Waving both his hands back and forth across his chest, he kept yelling, "No trade ... No trade," as he tried to get his saddle to fit back on his horse.

"Hey Ed, your nose is bleeding," Lou Smith called.

"Go to hell," Ed answered back. "Now let's git ... thataway," and he pointed to the northeast as Red Fox had done earlier.

As they rode out of the Indian camp, Red Fox called after them, in perfect English "Good by, gentlemen. Be sure to stop by again sometime."

Only Lou Smith looked back in amazement.

Chapter 12

It was late in the afternoon three days before Christmas when Red Fox came riding into the settlement. Although there was not much snow in the valley he had been forced to make his way through some of the passes between the Nez Perce winter camp and the settlement and Red Fox was near exhaustion when he arrived. They took him to London's new home and gave him hot tea with lots of sugar while food was being prepared.

A fire was burning in the huge fireplace and Red Fox's buffalo robe and his wolf and rabbit clothing was placed before it to melt the accumulated ice. Henri took charge of his mounts.

The big front room quickly filled with residents because they all knew that only trouble could force a person to travel alone in this kind of weather.

As soon as Red Fox was pretty much back to normal, he said, "Chief Ouseph has sent me to ask Colleen to come to our camp. Many of our children are sick and already some have died."

Colleen pushed through the crowd and sat down between London and Red Fox. "Tell me what you can," she said.

"About two weeks ago the children started getting sick and vomiting," Red Fox said. "All had very hot skin and a rash all over their bodies. Their bowel movements were weak and watery. Only a few of the adults got sick and they were not as hard hit as the children. The younger the child the more they seem to be affected and six children under the age of five years have died."

Colleen interrupted by asking, "Do they have sore throats?"

"Yes," Red Fox answered, "and after a few days they have like a red fur on their tongues and they are very weak. Often they rave and talk in their sleep like they are afraid of their dreams."

Colleen's face was pale as she said, "This is bad, very bad. I'll have to go to them at once."

"What do you think it is?" Helen asked.

"It could be a lot of things," Colleen said, "and I won't know for sure until I get there. Measles, whopping cough, scarlet fever or smallpox are all possible. My first guess would be scarlet fever since it seems to be affecting the children more than the adults. If it was smallpox everyone would be equally sick."

Delores Sanchez stepped forward and asked, "Are any of our children who are in your camp stricken with the sickness?"

"Yes, Delores," Red Fox answered, "I'm afraid your son is sick."

"Oh dear God!" she said as her hands went to her mouth and her eyes seemed to grow until they filled her face. "I must go to him!"

"Easy now," Roll spoke for the first time, taking charge. "We'll get a party ready to go tonight and they can leave the first thing in the morning. Colleen ... do you have the medicines you will be needing?"

"Our pharmacy is fully stocked so that won't be a problem," she answered. "I'll go now and start preparing my supplies."

"All right," Roll said. "Now let's decide who else will be going with Colleen. Are there any volunteers?"

Hands went up and voices shouted from all over the room.

"HOLD IT! ... WAIT A MINUTE!" Roll shouted. "We'll do this logically. Anyone with a child currently at the Indian camp will have first priority. Next I suggest Henri goes along with half a dozen Percherons to carry supplies and break trail for the other horses. London and Josh will go in case of trouble between here and there. Now let's make out a list of the rest of the volunteers and let Colleen choose who should go along. Women ride the lightest in most cases so they will have priority. They also make the best nurses."

"I'd like to go," Helen said stepping forward.

"No," Roll said and then explained by saying, "you're near as good a doctor as Colleen and we might need you here in case the sickness comes to the children in our camp. Now let's get busy preparing for the trip. Red Fox, you eat and rest so you can lead out in the morning."

From the supply room Roll brought garments best suited to winter travel, including long denim coats that reached from the hood on top to bottoms that fastened around each leg. The coats were double thick with goose down in between, warmer even than buffalo robes and a whole lot less weight to carry.

Dried fruit and beef jerky along with bacon, beans and potatoes were packed for food on the trail.

London had followed Colleen to where the medical supplies were kept and now he just stayed back out of the way and admired her professionalism.

Colleen's medical supplies had priority and each medicine was divided in half to be carried on two separate horses in case of an accident. Boracic acid, belladonna and arsenic were what she would use to fight the disease and she was praying it would be effective.

Helen joined Colleen and London in the supply room and asked, "Tell me, what do you think it is?"

"I'm afraid it's scarlet fever," she said. "If it's hitting the youngest children the hardest that would be a good indication. If it was small pox it would affect everyone and with measles there would be red spots. No mention was made of coughing so I think whopping cough is out. That leaves scarlet fever."

"That's exactly what I've been thinking," Helen said. "You and Josh have both had it so it shouldn't bother you to be with the sick children. But if we send anyone from here who hasn't had it they will most surely bring it back with them when they return."

"I think we should tell anyone who is going who has not had the fever that they will have to stay the rest of the winter in the Nez Perce camp to avoid contamination," Helen said. "That is unless you've got a better idea."

"The only other thing we could do is to only take people with us who have already had the disease," Colleen answered.

"That would work," Helen said, "but you might have to leave some of the parents of sick children here at the settlement."

"It would be preferable to bringing the disease back or leaving members of the party with the Nez Perce for the rest of the winter," Colleen replied.

"I'll go talk to Roll," Helen said, "and get his opinion. But if it turns out to be something other than scarlet fever all these precautions could be a waste."

"I had scarlet fever when I was a kid," London said, "so my going along won't be a problem."

Some time later as London was searching through the assortment of winter coats to find one to fit his lanky frame, Roll stopped at his side and said, "Maybe I was out of line to volunteer you to go along on this trip. You know you don't need to go if you don't want to."

"I like winter travel," London said with a smile.

"If you weren't here I'd go myself," Roll said. "I just want the party to have a solid leader in case of trouble. Colleen is my daughter and I worry … and … well, you know what I mean."

"Yes, I know exactly what you mean and she's not even my daughter," London said. "Don't worry, I'll watch out for her."

The caravan for the Indian camp started an hour before daylight to take advantage of the smooth traveling up the valley. The wind had swept most of the snow off to one side and the fifteen women and five men had it fairly easy except for the cold.

At that altitude and with the wind blowing mostly in their faces the brutal cold was hard on both horses and humans. Going up the valley they took turns leading the way. When the sun came up the glare from the snow was painful to the eyes so that only the person leading looked ahead. Everyone else just watched the horse in front. Even Red Fox had opted for one of the down filled coats and it was impossible to tell the men from the women in their identical garb with scarves wrapped around their faces.

On both sides of the valley the trees drooped heavily with the weight of the snow mashing down the branches. London knew from past experience that once they left the valley and entered the forests, the snow laden trees would gladly dump their burdens on the passing riders making travel even more difficult.

Once they had entered the trees, the lead rider kept a second horse at his side to help break the trail as well as the wind. The cold continued to be brutal.

They stopped briefly about noon to rest the animals. They made a small fire, not for heat but instead to boil water for hot tea to drink with the sandwiches they carried under their coats.

Now it was London's turn to lead and he used a fresh team of Percherons to break trail through the knee-deep snow. Off to the left of their direction of travel he could see smoke from the volcano and he used it as a guide to keep heading to the northeast. The party traveled steadily until sundown and then stopped at the first clearing in the forest to make camp for the night.

Caring for the animals, gathering wood, sweeping snow, hanging tents from trees and fixing food kept everyone busy for the first two hours. They built two fires, a small one for cooking and a big one for warmth. After eating they crawled into the tents and wrapped buffalo robes around their clothing and fell sound asleep, dead tired from the travel and the cold. Tomorrow would be more of the same agonizing pain for every mile of progress.

Colleen led out at first light. "I want to take my turn up front early so I can ride towards the back later on," she had said.

"Don't worry about that," London had said. "I'll take your turn leading."

"When are you going to learn?" she had said with a shake of her head.

"Okay," he had answered, "but you'll find a Percheron isn't as easy to ride as an Appaloosa. Anyway I just wanted to help."

"I can see where some of the really short women would have trouble," she said. "It would be okay if you and the other men want to help them out."

"Glad to," London said as he took his place in line.

The second and third day was exactly like the first and they made fair time over the frozen ground.

Towards the end of the third day Red Fox sought out London and Colleen and said, "Tonight should be our last night on the trail if it doesn't snow. Not far ahead is a large cave where we should all be able to spend the night. There is even room in the back for all the horses."

"When do you think we'll be at your camp?" London asked.

"My first night out I stayed in the cave I mentioned but I didn't leave our camp until noon or a little after. My guess would be early afternoon tomorrow," Red Fox said. "By using the big horses to break trail we made a lot better time coming back than I did getting to your settlement."

"Now I'm going up front," Red Fox said. "Delores Sanchez refused to let me take her turn leading so I'm going to ride the second lead horse and make sure she finds the cave."

Red Fox's prediction proved to be accurate and the next afternoon with Henri leading they crossed a ridge and saw the camp spread out below. They had seen smoke for the last two hours and it was spiraling straight up. The wind had settled that morning and the day was the warmest they had experienced since leaving the settlement.

A group of riders including Ouseph was riding out to meet them and Colleen pushed her horse forward, anxious to start helping the sick children.

Chapter 13

Two full weeks had gone by and Colleen was starting to control the epidemic. It was scarlet fever and very few of the adults were touched by the disease. All of the sick had been moved to the largest lodge and only Colleen and the nurses were allowed inside. A large hole had been dug about a mile from camp and any waste that came from the sick lodge was taken there and burned immediately.

The biggest problem had been keeping the patients warm 'but at the start of the second week a blizzard had howled out of the north and dumped more than three feet of snow on the camp. This covering had effectively insulated the structure where the sick were being kept and made heating it only a matter of many fires and keeping the smoke holes open in the roof.

Colleen worked twenty hours a day and slept in the sick house. Since her arrival only three children had died bringing the total of twenty-two children and four younger adults. The only positive from the sickness was that the ones who had been stricken and survived would be immune from the disease the rest of their lives.

London helped in every way he could and his admiration for Colleen's skill as a doctor grew with each passing day. She supervised everything and was available for any emergency. She even took time out to stitch up two Indian men who had been searching a cave for a mountain lion and actually found one.

Now Colleen was sitting on a blanket in the supply hut and London sat across from her. They were taking inventory of her medicines.

"You're the most amazing woman I have ever seen," he said.

"Maybe you're a little prejudiced," she replied.

"Of course I am. A man in love is expected to be," he said.

"Oh my," Colleen said. "As for my doctoring, I was just doing my job. As for being in love, I know exactly how you feel."

London leaned forward and took her hand while looking straight into her eyes. He had gone over this conversation a dozen times in his mind and now he was going to bring the subject out into the open. "You have a great gift," he said. "Have you ever considered going somewhere to put all of these skills to more generous use?"

"I'm useful here," she said.

"Yes you are," he answered, "but in a somewhat limited way. You could benefit so many more people if you made your skills available in a city."

"You mean leave the valley? Is that what you're trying to say?" she asked.

Now London asked the question that was the point of his whole conversation and steeled him self for the answer, "Have you ever thought about doing that?"

"I've thought of it a few times," she admitted, "but to leave my family ... I don't know if I could do that."

"Look," London said, "I promised your father that I would stay until spring and maybe even longer. Right now the only thing keeping me here is you."

"Do you mean that you intend to leave?" she asked.

"I can't live the rest of my life as a hermit in the mountains. Sooner or later people are going to come to this area and Roll will have to relax some of his rules. He'll have to share the marvels that he has created with the rest of the world."

"You may be right, I just don't know," Colleen said shaking her head and looking down at the blanket.

London reached out and put his fingers under her chin, raising her eyes so he could see into them. "You know I love you," he said, "but I want you to start thinking ..."

"And I love you," she interrupted.

"start thinking about life somewhere away from here," he finished.

"What would Father and Mother say?" she said. "You know very well how they feel about anyone leaving and not coming back."

"I'm not saying I would never come back," he said. "This is one of the most beautiful places I have ever seen. I'm just saying I'm not sure I want to spend the rest of my life here."

"I don't know ... I just don't know," she said. "If I told you I had never thought of leaving I'd be lying. Many times I have thought of how much good I could do someplace where I'm really needed."

"That's what I'm talking about," London said.

"But what of Father? Do you think he'd understand?" she asked.

"One way or another he'll have to accept it ... someone leaving, I mean," London replied, "because someday I will move on."

Colleen looked London straight in the eye and said, "You know you're forcing me to make a decision that I hoped I would never have to make."

"I'm sorry," he said, "but it is something you're going to have to think about. I never came here with the idea that I might fall in love. Now I'm as torn as you are."

"You do intend to stay until spring, don't you?" Colleen asked.

"At least that long," he answered.

"Maybe by that time the decision will be easier," she said.

London stood and took her hand pulling her to her feet as he said, "I hope it will be," but in his heart he knew it would only get more difficult with time.

Colleen bent down and picked up a bundle of supplies and took London by the arm. "Come on," she said, "there's work to be done in the hospital shelter."

Paths had been swept all through the camp and the snow was dazzling with the sun shining on it. They ducked out of the cold under the flap-door of the shelter containing her last seven patients, two of which were only babies and the others under six years old. They were all recovering and if she could keep them from pneumonia they should survive nicely.

Two Indian women and two women from the settlement were busy in the tent-shelter as they kept the fires going and made sure the children were warm.

London watched as Colleen went from bed to bed checking the children and talking quietly to the attending women. She walked back over to London and said, "Everything's fine for the moment. I'm going to lay down and take a short nap here in the hut so I'll be available in case something should change."

"That sounds like a really good idea," he answered. "I'll be doing the same thing over in the men's hut."

A week later they were on their way back to the settlement. They had left all of their medicines with the Nez Perce and the Indian women felt secure with the training they had received from Colleen.

There had not been a lot of new snow and now with the wind at their backs they made good time on the trail. Leading was no more work than following except it gave you a chance to change horses and on a long trip that was always welcome.

They pushed hard to get back, resting only four hours during the night and twice a day to eat and care for the horses. The whole party knew everyone back at the settlement would be extremely anxious for news from the Indian camp.

In spite of the cold and the many worries, Colleen and London were as happy as a couple of teen-age lovers. The only small cloud was London's name.

"Are you gonna' tell me or not!" Colleen demanded.

"I already told you," he said. "My name's London."

"Yeah," she replied, "but is it London something or something London? Which one is it?"

"What difference does it make?" he answered.

"It makes a difference to me!" she said irritably. "What did they call you in the army?"

"Sergeant," he replied.

"Very funny—ha-ha … very damn funny," and she rode on ahead in semi-serious anger.

When they finally made it back to the Escarpment all of the horses were left at the barn under the care of Henri and London. Roll had met them about half way up the valley and they had filled him in on the details of the mission.

There had been no unusual sickness while they had been gone so apparently the fever was going to miss their camp. Colleen felt sure that they had been gone long enough so none of the returning party should be contagious. Even so the children would avoid the exposed members of the community for another two weeks.

It was well after dark by the time London and Henri finished with the horses and made it to the main house where Roll waited for them.

"Well boys what'll it be first, food or a hot bath?" Roll asked.

"If you don't mind, I'm going on home," Henri said. "See you tomorrow," and with a wave he disappeared into the night.

"You suppose I could have a steak and potatoes while I soak in the bathtub?" London asked.

"Forget that!" Helen yelled from the kitchen doorway. "You get out here and eat what's on the table."

London walked into the kitchen and found a huge steak with all the trimmings waiting for him.

"As soon as I saw you ride in I started cooking," Helen said.

"Well I surely ain't gonna' let it go to waste," London said as he flopped down at the table and attacked the food.

Colleen came into the room and joined him at the table where Helen had placed a second steak. Strands of her reddish brown hair escaped from under the towel she had wrapped around her head. Her face was tanned and spotted from exposure to the sun, cold and wind of the last few days. Around her body was wrapped a long robe that reached clear to her ankles, provocatively exposing her bare toes as she walked with her long, country girl strides.

London caught his breath as he looked at her, once again sure that she was the most beautiful thing he had ever seen.

"I envy you," Colleen said to London as she sat down at the table.

"Why's that?" he asked.

"Because that hot bath I just finished has got to be one of the greatest experiences of my life and you still have yours ahead of you," she answered.

"You could be right but this meal isn't far behind," London said as he stuffed another chunk of super tender steak into his mouth.

"Food is going to be real plentiful for the next few days," Helen said, "now that you're all back safe and sound. We've got ham and turkey with all the extras saved over for our second Christmas dinner. As soon as you're up to it we're going to have another celebration."

"As long as we don't have to do it right away," Colleen said. "I plan to sleep for the next three days if that's okay with you," and her smile lit the whole room.

"That surely does sound good," London said. "Both the food and the sleep."

As they finished their meal the warmth of the room was starting to make the two travelers drowsy.

Colleen, who had finished her food, said, "I'll dash over to your house and fill the tub," and she pulled a coat over her robe and went out the door to run the short distance to London's house.

"That sounds mighty nice. I just hope I got enough strength left to climb out of the tub once I get finished," London said to no one in particular.

London walked into the house and could hear the water running. He took off his boots just inside the front door and walked towards the bathroom where he found Colleen bent over the tub adjusting the water temperature. The room was starting to fill with steam.

"There you go, fella," she said standing up straight and stepping back. "Get in."

"Like this?" he said looking down at his clothes.

"No." Colleen answered. "If I were you I'd get undressed before

I got in the tub."

"Whatever you say," he answered and began stripping off his clothes all the time watching her eyes appraising him. Naked, he stepped into the tub with the impression that she approved of what she was watching. He sat in the water and then stretched out, the tub being over six feet long. Taking a deep breath he allowed his head to go under the surface of the water and just soaked his entire body for as long as he could hold his breath. When he raised his head and opened his eyes Colleen was standing against the far wall of the room. She had been wearing only her robe with a coat over it and now those two garments were in a pile at her feet. He gasped for breath, breathing in four times before exhaling once.

"It only seemed fair," she said. "As I've told you before we should all do our duties equally."

London was slightly overwhelmed by the emotions of the moment. Dazzled by her perfection, he could only look and not speak. His eyes traveled from her reddish hair to her strangely provocative toes and back to her smiling eyes. He knew what this meant and he waited for her to speak.

"We're not children," she said, "but we live in a strange community. For now, this is enough. You understand anything more would put a terrible strain on everyone else in the settlement. We will have our time together, I promise you. That is the reason I'm standing here like this."

Colleen stooped down and gathered her robe up, wrapping it around her body and quickly topped it off by her heavy coat and said, "This way you know what's down the road, fella."

"You certainly know how to make things ... hummm ... how should we say, difficult," London answered.

"So I see," she said as she walked towards the tub, bent down and kissed him lightly on the mouth. "Now get a good night's sleep," she said as she went out the door and back to her own house.

Although it was still winter, there was still enough work to keep everyone busy. London was working on his story of the camp every day from noon until dark. In the mornings, he had been working in the kiln room molding and firing tile sewer pipes and roofs.

The smelter was running full blast making a new kind of twisted pipe to be used in the steam heating of the homes. Helen had designed a coil of pipes with a pressure release safety valve to be used in each room.

In the sawmill the crews were busy cutting and stacking lumber of all sizes to cure and be ready for spring building. Huge logs of cedar, walnut, oak, pine and redwood were brought daily by teams of horses over the frozen ground with the snow making the work somewhat easier.

Ice was cut from a nearby lake and hauled on skids to be stacked in the icehouse. Wheat was ground into flour in the gristmill and rags were made into blankets and rugs in the loom shop. Eggs were gathered, bread was baked and pigs were butchered and hung in the smokehouse. Beef, deer, elk, moose and buffalo were all processed into useable items. Soap and lard were rendered. All the inside repairs were finished and everyone waited for spring.

The mountain had been renamed Saint Helen and continued to smoke and rumble keeping the women on edge in spite of the fact that there had been no more earth tremors.

On this particular evening Josh, Colleen and London were eating dinner with Roll and Helen in their home.

"Even if there was any danger, which I'm sure there isn't, what could we do about it?" Roll was saying as they finished their evening meal.

"I understand that," Helen said irritably, "but it still worries me."

The volcano had been the main topic of conversation at dinner and that subject along with the winter's confinement had everyone a bit on edge.

"Let's change the subject," Colleen said looking at London. "How's the book coming along?"

"I think I've talked to everyone here in the settlement and have managed to get everyone's point of view," London said. "One other thing I would like to add to the book is the impressions of the Nez Perce and how your coming here has affected them. It would be an interesting sidelight to the story."

"I agree," Roll replied. "Ouseph and I have talked about it many times over the years but nothing was ever put down on paper. Knowing their feelings could be helpful to other settlers coming to this area in the future."

"Speaking of that," London said, "what are you going to do about this settlement when more people start coming into this area?"

Roll pushed back his plate, leaned forward and rested his arms on the edge of the table as he said, "I intend to go on just like we have been. I'm going to keep this valley private from outsiders."

"Have you considered with the growing population that some of the children who have been born here might want to move away and see more of the world?" London asked. "You know what I mean, beyond just leaving for an education and then returning here."

"After seeing the outside world why would anyone not want to come back here?" Roll said testily.

"I admit that this is a wonderful place to live," London said, "but there's also a lot to be said for life away from this valley."

Josh was listening intently to the conversation since he would be leaving in the summer to attend an engineering college back east.

Helen and Colleen were listening for different reason. The men were beginning to skirt the problem that they all had been dreading.

"You've seen the world away from here," Roll said to London. "What is there but man's inhumanity to man as someone once said?"

"That occasionally happens even here," London answered somewhat shortly.

"That's different," Roll answered back in much the same tone. "We try to stay to ourselves and not bother anyone. If we had been allowed to do that there never would have been any problems. Besides, everyone here knows the rules."

"You mean about leaving?" London asked.

"Yes! That and ALL the rest of the rules," Roll said back.

"Rules like Andersonville?" London asked softly, almost too softly to be heard.

Roll stared hard at London and was tense as he said, "Similar but different."

London leaned back in his chair not at all happy with the way the conversation was going. He chewed the inside of his cheek and rubbed his chin as he made up his mind. All the Jacobs family waited expectantly for him to say something.

"You know," London said in a perfectly normal tone, "I think when the weather breaks I should spend a week or two at Chief Ouseph's camp talking to him and the other elders. Their thoughts should be included in the history of this settlement."

Colleen and Helen let their breaths out slowly as the tension left the room. Josh also felt relief but he was not exactly sure why.

Roll nodded his head slowly and said, "That's a good idea. Knowing Ouseph like I do I'm sure he'll have a lot of insight that others would miss."

London took Roll's appeasing answer to mean that the discussion about leaving was over for now. But it had only been postponed.

Chapter 14

By the middle of April the outside temperature was just right to keep beer cool without freezing. A full barrel had been taped and was setting on London's front porch. It was Saturday afternoon and everybody in the settlement over the age of six had stopped by for a taste. Most of the men and a few of the women had had more than one sample of London's home brew.

There was a fire in the fireplace of London's front room and more than twenty people sat around filling all of the furniture and spilling over onto the floor.

Sean McNamara, being from Ireland, fancied himself something of a connoisseur and had sampled the beer at least a dozen times before admitting it was pretty good.

"Yes'sir London," Sean said, "this is the best beer I've had in many years. It's almost as good as what they got back in the old country. You've done a real good job in your brewery."

"Yep, I gotta' say it's a whole lot better than what they serve in town," London answered.

One of Colleen's younger sisters ran in the door and up to where Helen was sitting. "Mommy, can I have another glass, please," the girl asked in a child's pleading voice.

"No," Helen answered, "I think one is enough. Your Father said that anyone under ten years old gets one glass and those who are under fifteen get two."

"But Mommy, I'll be ten next month," she said.

"Oh go ahead," Helen said feeling pretty good herself, "but don't act silly and stay out of your Father's way."

Colleen and London were sitting on the stone hearth sipping their beer. "This is really good," Colleen was saying. "Where did you learn to make it?"

"There's a book in your father's library that has the instructions and when I was a kid still living with my parents I watched my father stir it up," London said.

"Oh, and what was his name?" Colleen asked hoping to catch London off guard.

"Gee, I don't know," London answered.

"You mean to tell me that you don't know your father's own name!?" Colleen almost shouted.

"Yep," London said with a big grin. "All I ever knew him by was 'Pa'."

"Mister, sometimes I don't like your crummy jokes," Colleen said, but then her face cracked into a smile and in spite of her resolve not to do so, she laughed.

"London," Helen shouted from the couch, "how's the book coming?"

"I'm done here at the settlement and if the weather holds I'll be going to see Ouseph next week and finish up that end of story," London answered.

"How long do you think that'll take?" Helen asked.

"Oh, three days there and three days back plus a week making notes at their camp ... a couple of weeks ought to do it." he said.

"Hey London," Josh called from across the room, "how about me going along? I'll be leaving for school back east in a couple of months and it would be my last chance to say good-bye to my friends there."

"You'd miss a lot of the spring plowing and planting," Helen said.

"Yeah, I know." Josh said with a grin.

"I'd welcome the company," London said.

Roll had just walked in from the porch with a fresh glass of beer in his hand. "What's this about missing the planting?" he asked.

"London is going to see Ouseph and Josh wants to go with him," Helen said.

"I don't see any problem with that," Roll said. "When are you planning on leaving?"

"The first nice day next week," London said. "I figure it'll take about two weeks."

"You say you WILL be back in a couple of weeks," Roll said with a slight under tone that only London, Colleen and Helen noticed.

"Absolutely," London answered, hearing very clearly what had NOT been said.

The ride from the Escarpment to Ouseph's camp had been extremely enjoyable. London and Josh rode from daylight to dark, stopping only at noon to eat and rest their horses. It had been a mild winter and new life was everywhere. Mountain goats and sheep, deer, antelope, elk, moose and all of the smaller animals were always in sight. The streams were full of otter, mink and beaver. On the second day they rode past a herd of buffalo that stretched for miles.

With no rain, cold or snow to bother them London and Josh rode into the Nez Perce camp on the afternoon of the third day. A delegation from the camp rode out to meet them again headed by Chief Ouseph who announced to the visitors, "Ho, London and Josh Jacobs, my friends, it is good to see you here at my camp."

"It is good to be here," London replied. "Much better than the last time."

"Yes," Ouseph answered. "How are the people at the settlement?"

"Everyone is fine," Josh said. "The fever missed us entirely."

Allowing their horses to walk, the group made their way slowly through the camp. Star had run out of her lodge when they went past and now she walked beside Josh's horse, chattering like a squirrel.

London turned to Ouseph and said, "We saw something yesterday that should be of interest to you, a huge heard of buffalo just north of where we fought the Cheyenne last year."

"That is good," Ouseph answered. "I will send riders to drive some of the beasts to our camp so that when they are killed we won't have far to carry the meat and skins."

"That makes sense," London said. "Josh would probably like to go along with them."

"I will ask him to go with our riders as a guide," Ouseph said.

"And there is something you can do for me," London asked. "Roll has asked me to write a history of the settlement at the Escarpment. I've talked to all of the settlers and now I would like for you and your people to tell me what they think of the white men coming into your country."

"I think that would be good for me and the others in this camp to express our feelings on the matter. You should eat and rest today. Tomorrow we will start the Chopunnish story," Ouseph said.

Ouseph and London were sitting on the bank of a large stream that meandered past the Indian encampment. London was busily taking notes as Ouseph talked. Red Fox and Morning were sitting with them.

"When the first wagon trains came to our country there was much discussion among our people as to what we should do," the Chief said. "All of the trains were only passing through this area and they didn't cause us any trouble so we adopted a wait and see attitude. A couple of trains had ended up at the Escarpment and had turned back looking for another route through the mountains. The third train was the one that had Roll and his party as members and they stayed in the valley."

"They built two large, crude houses to stay in that first winter," Ouseph went on, "and got along on the supplies they had brought with them. The first thing they did when spring came was to come to our camp in friendship. We were impressed that they did this and so we welcomed them as neighbors and Roll and I became friends."

Ouseph adjusted his seat on the blanket and went on with his story. "At first we warned them that the Escarpment was an evil place and they should not live in the shadow of the Rumbling Hills. At that time there was no smoke from the mountain and Roll said he was not afraid because the evil mountain was much too distant to cause trouble."

"We watched in wonder as Helen designed great machines and Roll built them. At first they heated boilers that supplied the steam power with wood burners and their first big achievement was a saw mill."

"Roll learned of the burning gas that comes from a crack in the hillside not far from the Escarpment and he came to me with the idea of trapping the gas in a tank and using pipes to bring it to the settlement for heat and light. The problem was how to make the pipe. We tried wood but it would not stand the pressure and the gas leaked away before it reached to shops and houses. Helen hit on the idea of casting pipe in the foundry but a workable metal was hard to find. Then, in the second year Helen suggested a gold/lead alloy that was soft enough to work but still strong enough to stand the pressure. This was how gas was first brought to the settlement. Soon it was used in their smelting plant and now they really began to progress."

London interrupted by saying, "What about your people? Did they see this as any sort of threat?"

"No, not at all," Ouseph said. "We just looked on it as people who lived differently from the way we live. It was during this time that Roll and I came up with the plan of exchanging children in order to break down the cultural and language barriers. Within a few years English and Chopunnish were common languages in both of our camps."

"Just before Roll left for the war, he and I decided that his settlement would have a set of rules governing strangers coming to visit. We both feared that the gold in these mountains would bring destruction to all of us."

"So you helped write the rules for the settlement," London said. "That is very interesting."

"So to speak, I guess I did," Ouseph said. Then he went on. "While Roll was gone Helen ran the settlement with the help of many of my people who aided with the crops and other chores. During this time we all learned a lot from each other."

"When the town was built south of here," Ouseph said, "no more wagon trains came this way. They were all directed to the proper trail through the mountains. After Roll returned from the war he decided to keep a guard at the only entrance to the valley and has done so ever since."

"What have been the biggest effects on your people?" London asked.

"For the most part," Ouseph answered, "it has been a welcome relationship. We have learned much from Roll and Helen. New foods and better clothing are two great benefits and Roll has discouraged travelers from coming to our country. He and I both encourage them to travel on through with no unnecessary stops."

"What other benefits have you seen?" London said.

"Probably the tools, cloth and firearms that Roll has been able to buy for us has been most beneficial," Ouseph said. "Axes, shovels, knives, rope and cooking utensils are all in everyday use. We trade him gold for these items and he takes it to Denver once a year and sells it without telling anyone where it comes from."

"And the school they run in the settlement seems to be beneficial to all the children," London said.

"I'm sure that in times to come more white people will be arriving in this country," Ouseph said. "I would like for my people to be prepared to meet them on an equal basis of understanding. Roll has even tried to get me to send some of my people back east for further education."

"Are you going to do it?" London asked.

The Chief turned to Red Fox and said, "Tell him how you feel about this."

"We have discussed education and for now we are against it," Red Fox said. "There are only a few things that would benefit our people such as medicine and possibly engineering. In order for further education in other fields to be useful our whole style of life would have to change."

"Do you think this is going to happen?" London asked.

"Not in the near future," Red Fox said. "Perhaps in years to come we will need to do this but for the present everything is fine."

"Not even to have your own teachers?" London replied.

Chief Ouseph's head snapped up and he looked intently at London. "That is one thought we have never discussed," he said. "It could be that we might have overlooked something."

The next day London spent in the company of Star, Red Fox and Morning. They told London of the time they spent at the Escarpment, a place of evil spirits to their people. Red Fox had been among the first exchange group and the two women among the second group.

"The settlers paid very little attention to the Rumbling Hill," Red Fox said. "Of course we had been raised to fear this part of the country and every time the volcano acted up the Indian children would want to run and hide. The settlement children would heckle us when we did this so finally we learned to accept the volcano for just what it is, a natural phenomenon."

"Not entirely," Star interrupted. "The women of the settlement were much more cautious than the men. When there were earth tremors they would be frightened and their fear was communicated to the girls in the camp."

"I see," London said making notes as they talked. "Besides the volcano what was the biggest difference between the camps for the children?"

"The daily routine," Morning said. "Here we have work and chores that must be done every day and very little time to play and have fun. There we went to school, always inside, for several hours a day and for our people being cooped up was very uncomfortable. As we adjusted to our schedule we found that we actually had more play time there than in our own camp. We had chores but not nearly as many as at home."

"What were the main problems caused by the exchange?" London asked.

"The different life styles was the hardest adjustment for me," Red Fox said and the two women nodded in agreement.

"As the years went by," Star said, "the settlement had warm houses with floors and lights for the darkness. Hot and cold running water and inside toilets and the most important advantage to women, privacy."

"Does this mean you preferred one life style over the other?" London asked.

"No, I can't really say that," Morning answered. "Each camp had its good points and some not so good. For me it was very difficult to learn the white man's reading and writing. Others learned much quicker than I did."

"Do you think the exchange of children is good?" London asked.

All three nodded in agreement as Star said, "Oh yes, all of this has gone to make life better for both camps."

"How about further education?" London asked. "Do you think that would be good?"

Star answered quickly by saying, "The thought of going to school to learn to be a teacher is very appealing to me. Since I first heard it mentioned last night I have thought of nothing else."

"Do you think Chief Ouseph would approve of such a thing?" London said.

"Yes," Red Fox replied. "After our conversation along the stream he spoke very positively about Indian teachers for Indian children."

"Hey! … Hey! … Hey!" Josh yelled as he walked towards the group.

"What's all the noise about?" Red Fox asked.

"A bunch of us are going out to try to drive some buffalo close to camp. We're leaving this afternoon," Josh said.

"Yeah, I know," Star said. "I'm going too."

"Are you going?" Josh asked London.

"No, I want to interview a few more people here at the camp, especially your doctor," London answered.

"Then how about for now we …" Josh started to say when the

ground began to tremble and they all turned their eyes to the skyline.

The smoke grew thicker and darker even as they watched. The first tremor was followed by another and still another, so many that they lost count.

When the sound finally reached them from that great distance, it sounded like muted thunder or a low continuous beating of drums. Everyone who had been inside was now outside and looking to the northwest. Soon the tremors stopped and the noise ceased but they could still see the flames and smoke shooting into the sky.

Chief Ouseph joined London and the rest. "This is bad," he said. "It has been many years since the Rumbling Hills have been so loud. I may be called a superstitious old man but when the mountains shake I feel fear in my heart."

"But there's nothing we can do, is there?" Josh asked

"No, my friends," Ouseph said, "only wait and see what the future brings." It was obvious to all that the Chief was deeply troubled.

Chapter 15

It was late in the afternoon when London and Josh rode back into the settlement. Roll, Helen and Colleen were waiting on the front porch of their house and Josh was so excited he didn't get dismounted before he yelled, "Hey, guess what? Star is going back east with me to go to school. How about that!"

"Tell us more," Colleen said as Josh slid from his horse and ran up the front steps.

"London and Ouseph were talking and London mentioned that Indian teachers would be best for Indian children. Anyhow Ouseph talked it over with the other Elders and they decided to send Star to school back east. She's leaving when I do if the arrangements can be made," Josh said.

"That's great," Colleen said. "Star is probably the best student we ever had here at our school."

"We do have a lot to talk about," Roll said. "How about after dinner we all sit down and discuss everything. While you were gone we had more tremors here and we'll fill you in on that and you can tell us about your progress on the story of the settlement."

"Sure, be glad to," London said, "but now I want to get in the bathtub and soak for an hour. I never knew how much I could miss a hot bath."

"I'll walk over with you," Colleen said, "and wait for you to get the trail dirt washed off before I give you a kiss."

"You go on in and get cleaned up too," Roll said to Josh. "I'll take the horses up to the corral."

"Wait," Josh said. "Ouseph sent you something in my saddle

bags. He thinks there should be enough gold to cover the expenses of Star going to school. If it's not enough, let him know. If it's too much just apply it to the cost of the store goods he ordered."

"Okay, I'll let him know," Roll said as he tossed the bags on the porch and headed for the corral with the horses.

Colleen and London headed for his house and as soon as they were out of earshot of anyone else Colleen said, "There's something we have to discuss," and just from the tone of her voice London could tell it was not going to be something he wanted to hear.

"I told Mother and Father that I'm in love with you," Colleen said.

"What was their reaction to that?" London asked.

"I'm sure they have known for some time what was what along those lines," she answered. "But when I said we might decide to leave the settlement neither one took it very well."

"Go on," London said as he opened the door to his house and they went inside.

"I'm going to tell you straight out what was said and I hope you won't think I'm being forward. The first thing Mother said was were we planning a wedding or had any mention be made of such a thing."

London smiled and said, "You know that is what I want but this is not exactly how I planned to propose."

"I know and I understand. But now I'm telling you what was said without leaving anything out," Colleen said. "My parents didn't react the way I expected."

"Good or bad?" London asked.

London had sat in a chair, the bath postponed by this important talk.

Colleen stood at the fireplace and looked at him with tears in her eyes and said, "Bad ... real bad."

"Tell me all of it," London asked.

Colleen took a deep breath and said much too quickly, "Mother and Father have agreed. We won't be allowed to leave the settlement."

London said nothing for at least a full minute. He looked around the room at the perfect surroundings, the beautiful woman and out the windows that showed the view over the edge of the Escarpment. He took several slow, deep breaths as his mind processed everything he saw and put it together with what he had just heard.

"In spite of what your parents have said, that decision is as much up to us as it is to them. Even more up to us, really," London said looking up at Colleen. "Since I have not had a chance to talk to Roll and Helen about this, nothing, and I do mean nothing has been decided," London said adamantly.

"What do you plan to do?" Colleen asked.

London could see how upset Colleen was and tried to take some of the tension out of the conversation. "I intend to discuss this with your parents and then I am sure we will be able to find some middle ground that will help us all find a reasonable solution."

"Do you think you really can?" Colleen said walking to his chair.

"Yes ma'am, I do," London said rising to his feet. "Now trail dirt or not, I want that kiss here and now."

He got it and much, much more.

Dinner that evening for Roll, Helen, Josh, Colleen and London was cordial but somewhat subdued. Roll had been doing most of the talking as he told London and Josh of how the last earth tremors had effected the settlement. The ditch that had opened the previous fall had reopened and both gas and sewer lines had been broken. None of the damage had been very severe and everything had returned to normal operation in less than three days.

Now they had adjourned to the porch with their coffee and were discussing the schedule for the next couple of months. They had agreed that Roll and Helen would accompany Josh and Star as far as Denver and Colleen and London would accompany the wagons and return with them to the settlement. The wagon train would go as far as town with the travelers and Henri and Miguel would handle the wagons and pick up supplies in town. Red Fox, Morning and at least twenty of the Nez Perce would be coming with Star and would stay with the wagons, escorting them back to the Escarpment.

Since they would be a relatively small party going to Denver, Roll was going to take two of the Percheron horses with him and they would be loaded with beaver pelts. Hidden in among the skins would be the gold they would be carrying to Denver. All four would be well armed with six-guns and one of the new Winchester rifles waiting at the store. Before starting back, Roll would sell three of the extra horses and keep one for supplies so that he and Helen could travel light and fast on the return trip. If they had no difficulties they should be back in about three weeks.

"That's it then," Roll said. "Do these arrangements suit everyone?"

"I'm a little concerned about you and Mother traveling alone through the Cheyenne country," Colleen said.

"We've done it many times before," Helen said. "Remember that your father and I aren't a couple of greenhorn kids. We can take care of ourselves."

"What's next on the agenda?" London asked, hoping Roll would want to know if he had anything to add.

No such luck as Roll continued to talk saying, "In the last letter I got from my brothers in Philadelphia they mentioned that a new college was opening near their home. The school is called Swarthmore and it's supposed to have an exceptional engineering school. I'm sending them a letter suggesting that our family make an endowment to help get the school started. This should serve the purpose of assuring admittance to any of our children who are seeking education and guarantee fair treatment for anyone of the family that would chose to attend. Also anyone from here would have our family to live with while they were attending classes."

This time it was Roll who said, "Anything else need talking about?"

"Yes there is," London said. "I think we need to talk about the rules you have for the settlement. I don't know if this is the best time but we've been hedging around the subject for a good while now and

I think we should try to come to some sort of understanding."

As soon as London started to speak Roll turned towards Colleen with a stern look of disapproval.

London was prepared for the conversation that followed. He had thought about it every day for months and was ready to answer any of Roll's questions. London was going to take a stand and Roll and Helen would have to allow him to have his say.

"Roll, when I came here last year at your invitation you never qualified it to mean that I would become a prisoner once I arrived," London said. "I believed I was coming to visit an old friend. Now we're in something of a situation."

London paused for a few seconds to allow anyone who wished to say something but nobody spoke so he went on. "You explained the rules of the settlement to me and I understood them and the reasons for having these guidelines and that was what I thought they were. I never imagined that we would reach the impasse we are at here today."

London stopped again and looked at Roll as he said, "Do you agree so far?"

"Go on talking," Roll said somewhat impatiently. "It's your turn."

"The last thing I could have expected was to meet Colleen and fall in love. Now you've put us both in a nearly impossible position. We want to get married and live our own lives and you've said we can get married but we have to live according to your rules. Do you really expect us to do this?" London asked.

Roll took a deep breath and said, "I'm going to try and understand what you are telling me. But I want you to know that what we are discussing are rules and not just guidelines. Possibly there is a middle ground. I've listened to what you have to say and I want to respect the feelings of my daughter as well as your own concerns. Now I have a question for you. Is there any particular rush to come up with a solution?"

"Not really," London answered. "Any reasonable length of time would suit us just fine."

"What would you say to getting this trip to town out of the way, the trip to Denver finished and the kids off to school," Roll said. "By that time Helen and I will have had time to discuss everything and come up with some sort of offer."

"That sounds fair to me," London said and he looked at Colleen and said, "How about you?"

Colleen was all smiles when she said, "Oh yes. I've been so worried thinking about what to do I just ... well ... now that we're talking I'm sure it's going to be all right."

Roll turned to Helen and said, "Did you have anything you wanted to add?"

"No," she said. "Like Colleen I'm just happy we're going to come up with a solution."

~~~ Chapter 16 ~~~

It had been a year since London had arrived at the settlement and it was time for the annual visit from the Nez Perce. London and Colleen stood on the porch of his house and watched the party ride in. The Indians were all dressed in their finest clothing as was their custom. As they dismounted and started to circulate at the food tents, Star broke away and guided her horse to where London and Colleen were watching the new arrivals.

Before getting off her horse she reached down and removed her white moccasins and then ran bare footed up the steps of the house. She was shaking with excitement as she grabbed London with one hand and Colleen with the other and said, "Tell me about back east. I've got a thousand questions and I want them all answered right now!" and all three laughed.

"I can't tell you anything about the school you'll be attending," Colleen said "because this is its first year of classes. I know it is less than three miles from where our relatives live there in Philadelphia so transportation won't be a problem."

"Who will I be staying with while I'm there?" Star asked.

"You and Josh will both be staying with our father's brother. He's an attorney in Philadelphia and he will help you get settled."

London sat in a chair watching and listening to the women talk. When Star asked her next question he listened intently to Colleen's answer.

"Do you think the people there will accept me ... you know ... being an Indian?" Star asked.

"Of course they will," Colleen said. "This isn't the dark ages and you're a beautiful woman. I'm sure the boys at that school will notice this right away."

London kept his thoughts to himself but he had reservations about Colleen's last answer. There were still a lot of people living that could remember the bloody Indian wars back east and the tension between the new settlers in the west and the powerful Indian tribes of the areas was a topic of daily news. London felt that the dealings with the Nez Perce here in their own environment and the relations between the Indians and the residents of this settlement did not adequately prepare Star for the hostility she would confront when she entered white society. In fact London had been none too fond of Indians before his arrival at the settlement. In his heart he wished Star good luck but realistically he knew she was in for a hard time.

London abandoned his thoughts and went back to listening to the conversation between the two women.

"What about clothes and things like that?" Star asked.

"Mother has taken care of it," Colleen answered. "She sent a note with father's letter to uncle's wife telling her to make arrangements for a dressmaker to be available to fit you with the latest wardrobe." Then Colleen indicated the white moccasins in Star's hand and said, "Back there you don't need to take your shoes off to keep from getting them dirty."

"That's just a habit with my dress-up clothes," Star said. "Now tell me about the men back there and how I should act?"

London perked up at this question and started to pay close attention, something both women noticed immediately.

"Come with me," Colleen said leading Star into the house. "We need some privacy to discuss this topic."

As the two women disappeared through the front door, Colleen turned to London, made a face crossing her eyes and stuck out her tongue. "Not for your ears, buster," she said, "we girls still have a few secrets."

The warm breeze from the south made it a pleasant evening to sit on London's front porch. There were more than twenty people scattered about, talking and laughing as they enjoyed the summer weather. It was the third day since the arrival of Ouseph and his people and all of the usual summer business had been completed. The next morning everyone would be leaving.

Most of Ouseph's people would be returning to their camp. The wagons going to town would be back in a little over a week, Roll and Helen would return in three or four weeks and Josh and Star would not be back for three or four years. It was a sad and happy time all rolled into one.

"I'm glad the rumbling hills are quiet," Ouseph said to London. They were sitting on London's front steps. "It worries me when there is fire and smoke in the air and the ground shakes," Ouseph went on.

"It seems peaceful enough now," London said. "If we could just get Star settled down everything would be perfect."

Ouseph smiled at his joke. All the white settlers had been cornered by Star in the last couple of days and interrogated about their knowledge of life beyond the mountains. She had especially bothered London for information about the riverboats. She had been so demanding that Roll had promised her she could take a boat from St. Louis to Pittsburgh. From there she and Josh would ride the train on to Philadelphia.

"You know about the surprise Roll has arranged for Star in Pittsburgh?" London asked Ouseph.

"No, what's that?" Ouseph asked.

"Josh will send a telegraph ahead to Roll's brothers and arrange for them to have their private railroad car waiting for Star and Josh in Pittsburgh," London said. "I was told that Roll and Helen own a large share of the railroad on which they'll be riding."

There was a slight commotion at the corner of the house and London and Ouseph turned to see Sean McNamara and Roll come around the corner with a barrel of beer on a handcart. In spite of the imminent separations, this would boost everyone's spirits and help

146

relax the mood.

Helen and Colleen made a quick trip to the barrel and then joined London and Ouseph on the steps as Helen was asking "Is there anything you want us to bring you from Denver?"

"Nothing but the list of medicines that I gave you," Colleen answered.

"You can get me something," London said. "I need some new decks of cards. The ones we have here almost have the spots worn off."

Roll joined them with three mugs of beer, handing one to Ouseph and the other to London.

"That should be easy enough," Helen said. "How about you, Ouseph, is there anything you would like from the city?"

Ouseph shook his head slightly and said, "No, everything we need we get in town or here at this settlement. We need nothing more."

"You're sending a lot of gold with me," Roll said. "Do you want me to bring back gold coins for you or put your money in the bank?"

Ouseph and Roll had discussed this question many times over the years and Ouseph, after much thought, always had Roll bring him gold coins for his nuggets. Over the years Ouseph had placed so many coins in a bag back at his camp that it was more than three strong men could lift. Nobody had the slightest idea of what he planned to do with the money. Paying the expenses for Star to attend school would be the first money he had ever spent except for supplies in town or what money he spent with Roll.

"Like always," the chief said, "bring coins and I will take some to camp and leave some with you to spend at the store."

"How about the little rifles?" Roll asked.

"Yes, I nearly forgot," Ouseph said. "My men like them very much. I think twenty more of them would be good. Can you have them sent to the store in town so you won't be burdened coming back?"

"Certainly," Roll answered. "Is that all?"

"Bullets for the little guns," the chief said.

"I'll have them shipped with the rifles," Roll replied.

The conversation lagged as everyone rested on the porch watching the sun go down past the Escarpment. Colleen and London sat on the top step, her head on his shoulder and his arm around her waist.

For five full minutes it was quiet and then Star came running up and said to London, "Tell me again about the riverboats."

In deference to the Cheyenne raid the year before, when the wagons reached the entrance to the valley, Ouseph sent two of his men accompanied by Miguel Sanchez ahead as advance scouts. They were to stay about an hour ahead of the wagons.

It had been fairly dry and the wagons were making good time on the firm ground. There were no unusual interruptions and the wagons reached town on the evening of the third day.

Dinner that night was a somber affair particularly for Josh and Star. Neither had been further than this tiny town and here was just the first step of a journey that would carry them more than half way across the continent.

Star was anxious for many reasons but most of all she would be the first representative of her tribe to go into the white man's world. She was afraid she would fail and be disgraced. Now she sought out London and Colleen and confided her fears.

"The night before we left the settlement," Star said, "Helen took me aside and told me not to be afraid. She said that when Roll wanted to go west, she was scared to death. She said she had been afraid she would fail her new husband. She had feared the wild animals and the even wilder Indians that lived there. I couldn't imagine Helen being scared of anything and her talk helped to cheer me up. She said she learned that most of her fears were foolish and she came to love this country. Helen told me that while I might not learn to love the east, she was sure I would conquer my fears and be just fine."

Colleen put her arm around Star and said, "London and I have talked about this and we both feel you won't have any trouble adjusting but that if you do, Josh and the rest of our family will be there for you."

London said nothing. He had already conveyed his concerns to

Colleen and saw no reason to bring them up to Star and cause her more worry.

The next day the wagons pulled up to the general store and began loading supplies. Roll paid the storekeeper and then opened one of the cases of Winchesters and removed four of the rifles. He and London sat on the back of one of the wagons and cleaned away the factory grease and loaded the weapons. Roll put two hundred extra rounds of ammunition on one of the packhorses and was ready to head for Denver. All the farewells having been said, Roll, Helen, Josh and Star headed out.

The wagons had made it back to the Escarpment without incident and all the supplies belonging to the Nez Perce had been sorted out and loaded on a string of packhorses for transport. The Indians would keep the horses at their camp until their next visit to the escarpment. Chief Ouseph and his people had departed the following day.

A week had gone by without any activity from the volcano and on this morning London and Colleen were eating breakfast on the front porch of Helen and Roll's house. They were sharing an eight-egg omelet made with chopped bacon and fresh onions. London had done the cooking.

"That food's not bad for an amateur cook," Colleen said.

"The secret is not getting the stove too hot," London answered. "If we could figure out a way to keep constant heat like maybe using that gas for cooking, I could be an even better chef."

Colleen stared and said, "There you go again. This idea might be even more important than your steam heat. As soon as I tell mother what you said she'll have something designed and father will turn one out in the machine shop within a week."

"You give me more credit than I deserve," he said. "I was just supposing about the stove. Hey, look, a rider's coming from the barn. I wonder what's up?"

It was unusual for Henri to run a horse that hard. He skidded to a stop at the porch and vaulted to the ground yelling, "GRIZZLY! ... AFTER THE HORSES ... Big female with two near full grown cubs at the corral!"

"Get a couple more men and meet me back here," Colleen yelled at Henri as she turned and ran into the house. "We need bigger guns than the Winchesters."

London was right behind her as they ran to the gun rack in the front room and each grabbed three of the big fifty caliber Sharps rifles and a hand full of shells and were back out the door in a flash. Colleen veered off towards a field beside the house where two teams of Percherons were pulling hay rakes. "Cut those horses loose so we can have something to ride!" she yelled. "There's grizzly bears after the horses at the corral!"

The men plowing pulled the harnesses from the Percherons and jumped onto their broad backs, each accepting a rifle and shells from Colleen and London as they climbed aboard the other two horses.

Henri had located two more men and London quickly passed out the last of the big rifles and the race was on for the barn and the bears. Henri and the men he had found were mounted on Appaloosa horses and they quickly outdistanced the others.

When Henri reached the barn two boys were standing in the loft door and pointing around the corner. "They're right down there, almost in the barn!" one of the boys yelled frantically.

"Stay up there out of the way," Henri shouted back. "We'll handle it."

Henri's feet had hardly touched the ground when the huge she-bear came around the corner and stood up on her hind feet to survey the situation. There was a board fence between the bear and the men but the bear was easily twice as tall as the fence. All three men were now on the ground looking up at the bear less than fifty feet away.

"Don't miss!" Henri yelled at the others as he brought his gun to his shoulder and fired.

His bullet hit her square in the middle of her chest and feeling pain, rage, and fear she dropped on to all fours and charged through the fence as if it were made of straw.

The other two men fired as Henri was reloading. One bullet struck the bear's left foreleg and the other hit her in the head, momentarily stopping her. Henri's second shot went straight down her throat, finishing her.

Now the two younger bears, both as large as their mother came around the corner and charged through the break in the fence.

"RELOAD—HURRY!" Henri yelled.

All three men fired at the same time and unwittingly they all aimed at the same bear which collapsed in its tracks.

London, Colleen and the other two men arrived just as the third bear reared up over the men on the ground. At the sight of the bear the horse London was on spun around and bucked all at the same time throwing him directly into the bear's path. He landed flat on his back, stunned and helpless. All he could see from the ground was the huge, dark apparition standing over him. A shadow passed in front of his eyes and for an instant he thought it was death. In fact it was life.

Colleen stood astride his body and fired her shot directly up into the bear's face. The bullet went in through the chin and out the top of the bear's head knocking it backwards and killing it without a quiver.

London was more than a little shaky as he climbed to his feet. "I guess I better stick to cooking breakfast and let you handle the bears," he said as he got his breath back.

"I think a bear skin rug will look nice in front of your fireplace," Colleen answered.

That evening at London's house they sat and talked.

"When I saw you working with the sick children at the Indian camp I realized how valuable your skills were," London said. "Twice since I've been here you could have been killed and it scares me. I've never been afraid before in my life but now, because of you, everything has changed."

London was sitting on the floor at Colleen's feet and he hugged her legs as he went on. "I want you to marry me and return to the city where you can practice your trade."

Colleen reached down and put her fingers in his hair, rubbing his head as she took a deep breath and sighed it out. "I haven't thought of anything else in a long time," she said, "and I'm so torn over the decision."

"I know your father wants me to stay," London replied, "but sooner or later I want to go back to the city. The thing with the bears today has made me more aware of the dangers here in the mountains. Maybe I'm being selfish but I want to take you somewhere safe."

"I understand how you feel," she said, "but the thought of leaving the settlement and my family is overwhelming. I love you and want to marry you but the idea of leaving is ... oh, I just don't know ... I just ... oh, what to do, what to do?"

Colleen slid from her chair onto the floor at his side turning her face to be kissed, turning her body to be held.

Chapter 17

Peter Digondo was the guard at the head of the valley when Roll and Helen returned. He immediately flashed the pre-arranged signal to the settlement and London and Colleen met her mother and father half way to the Escarpment.

"How was your trip?" were the first words out of Colleen's mouth.

"It was wonderful," Helen said. "We never had a vacation before. It's been like a second honeymoon."

"That's great," Colleen replied. "You both deserved some time off to relax and enjoy yourselves."

"Anything special happen while we've been gone?" Roll asked.

"Well, sort of," Colleen answered with a laugh. "London has all the makings for three great big bearskin rugs."

"How's that?" Helen said.

Colleen launched into the story of the three bears and did her best to minimize the danger of the situation. She finished by saying, "and we never did find a Goldilocks."

"You make it sound almost like fun," Roll said seriously. "It sounds to me like we were damn lucky nobody got killed."

"You can say that again," London said. "If it hadn't been for Colleen ... well, you heard the story."

A large crowd had gathered around Roll and Helen's house and a large keg of beer that had been kept in the icehouse now rested in the front yard on a couple of sawhorses. As soon as everyone had a mug and a chair Roll began telling the story of the trip to Denver.

"Even traveling at the slower speed of the pack horses," Roll said as he started his story, "we were making good time. I have traveled this route many times in the last decade or so and it was easy to find the best river crossings and campsites. Game was abundant and we had grouse, rabbit, squirrel and fish whenever we wished. About the fourth day or so we came on a herd of buffalo. As you all know, where there are buffalo there are also other critters aplenty, some of them two legged. Not wanting to advertise our passage we made a hard right turn towards the mountains and circled wide around the herd. Nine days after we left the wagons we were in Denver, sunburned, tired and ready for a bath."

"Helen went off to get us rooms in the hotel and Star went with her. Josh and I went to the bank and that was where his education began," Roll said.

"At the bank Josh got his first lesson," Roll went on. "We got the gold that was hidden among the beaver hides and went into the bank. I asked to see the bank's president and they asked who we were. When I gave the teller our names he ran for the back of the bank like his rear end was on fire and Josh couldn't figure out what was going on. When the president came out and said how happy he was to see us Josh was even more mystified. As soon as we were alone with the man in his office, Josh discovered that the bank president, Linus Ford, actually worked for us and that we were the secret owners of the bank."

"I didn't know you owned the bank in Denver," London whispered to Colleen.

"Oh yes, that and lots of other things," Colleen confided back. "Your future wife is from a very well-to-do family."

"After we finished our bank business," Roll continued, "Josh's education continued. We walked across the street to the hotel and the manager and two bellboys were waiting to escort us to our rooms. Helen had announced our arrival and the three best suites were ready and waiting, one for Josh, one for Star and one for Helen and I. That was when Josh found out we also own the hotel. After we got to the room I told Josh that the bank manager was also the supervisor of all our holdings in Denver. We had hired him back in Philadelphia through my brothers and brought him here just for that purpose."

"Star was having the time of her life," Helen said interrupting Roll's narrative. "She had seen nice furniture here at the settlement so that didn't impress her as much as the service we were receiving from the bustling employees of the hotel as they rushed about providing every service. Flowers, snacks, drinks and bathtubs full of hot water seemed to appear out of thin air. Star was still wearing her Indian clothing and this drew a few curious stares but everyone knew that we were the real bosses so they were all most gracious."

"That evening," Roll went on after a big swallow of beer, "we had dinner in the hotel dining room with the bank manager and our attorney there in Denver. They filled us in on all of the latest news and told us that they would take care of all the arrangements for Josh and Star to travel to Philadelphia."

"Oh, and one other thing we did," Helen said, "was to set up a surprise for Star when the train they would be on reached St. Louis. Without telling her we made arrangements for them to travel by riverboat from St. Louis to Pittsburgh and from Pittsburgh to Philadelphia in a private railroad coach. Both of our families are major stockholders in the B & O Railroad and our family has a private coach for whenever they wish to travel."

Colleen shot an elbow into London's ribs and gave him her cross-eyed grin as she whispered, "Ya' see fella, you're really going to get your money's worth."

Roll was still talking and announced to everyone that when the spur line had been finished into Denver it had become possible to board a train there and go all the way to either New York or San Francisco without ever stepping back on the ground.

Sean McNamara spoke up and said, "The way you talk about them building railroads, how long will it be before we'll be able to hear the whistle?"

"A very long time, I hope," Roll answered, with a scowl. "It may be called progress but we don't need that kind of foolishness around here."

The party went on for several more hours but Roll and Helen, worn out from travel, were among the first to call it a night.

London sat alone on the front porch of his house. The moon was bright enough to cast shadows on the ground and the air was unmoving and filled with the night sounds of crickets. He was puzzling over the talk Roll had given earlier in the evening. For a man who was basically very secretive, Roll had revealed more then London would have ever thought possible. What had been his reason for all of those revelations? London thought he knew. London thought Roll had been speaking directly to him and had said in a round about way, do you want to be a rich man? Then stay here, marry my daughter and do as you've been told.

London had not had a chance to discuss his conclusions with Colleen and he would be very interested in what she thought.

Before Roll had gone into the house he had called London aside and told him that there was something very important he wanted to talk about the next day. London was sure Roll would be making an offer of some kind to get him to stay in the valley and he wondered in what way he would be tempted. The new facts that Roll and Helen were a couple of the richest people in the United States put a new twist on things.

Money alone was not that important to London. He had enough put away to live comfortably for two or three years. Now he had learned that his money was in a bank belonging to Roll, Helen and, in essence, his fiancé.

London looked across the open ground in front of him, over the Escarpment and into the night sky. Again he was nearly overwhelmed by the breathtaking beauty. This was THE most beautiful place on earth.

Would he, or better yet, could he compromise enough to go along with Roll's wishes. For a few more minutes he sat and then, his mind made up, he got up and walked into the house. One way or the other he would be moving on before winter and Colleen would be going with him.

Colleen walked onto the porch, a cup of coffee in her hand. Her parents were still in bed. Out near the rail fence along the edge of the Escarpment she was surprised to see London and what appeared to be a kitchen chair sitting beside him. The chair was covered with objects but from fifty yards away she could not tell exactly what they were. She returned to the house and poured a second cup of coffee and now with a cup in each hand she headed to where London stood. As she got closer she could see he was wearing his gun belt and the chair was covered with boxes of cartridges and two rifles leaned against its back.

As soon as London became aware of her approach he stopped fussing with the equipment on the chair and just watched her approach.

"Good morning," he said as she handed him the coffee. "That was mighty sweet of you," and he kissed her on the cheek.

"What on earth are you up to?" she said curiously.

"Just something I like to do but haven't done lately. You know I like guns and shooting and I just thought I'd play for a while," he said. "It would be nice if you'd stick around and watch."

"I'd like that," she answered.

London bent over and picked up a sack that was on the ground beside the chair and walked to the rail fence. He reached in the sack and took out six half grown green apples and lined them up on the top rail of the fence. Then he walked back towards Colleen counting his steps out loud, "seven … eight … nine … ten," and he turned so he was facing the fence and took the keeper thong off the hammer of the six gun he was wearing at his side. He turned and looked at Colleen with a big smile and then once again faced towards the fence.

Maybe it was the noise that was most startling. There was no bang, bang, bang of shots going off, just one loud roar and the apples were gone. Six shots fired in an instant and six hits. London had put his empty gun back in the holster before Colleen even knew he was ready to shoot. She stood with her mouth open in amazement and stared.

"My God, what was that!" she said breathlessly. "I've never seen anything like it."

"Just practice," London said. "Sorry about not telling you to cover your ears. The noise can be a bit disturbing."

"Can you do that every time?" she asked.

"Yeah, about," he said. "Sometimes I might miss one but I haven't missed two in a long time. You want to see some more?"

"Oh yes, please," she said.

"Okay," London said, "this is how it goes," and he started to reload his revolver. "Back on the riverboat the passengers sometimes got a little bored and I would go to the back of the boat and put on kind of an exhibition. We would get a couple young fellas to throw things in the air and I'd shoot at them with both revolvers and rifles. Like this!"

London bent over and grabbed three apples in his left hand and in one motion threw them into the air. Boom-Boom-Boom and they were gone.

"Amazing!" Colleen said, as she was suddenly joined by a crowd of residents from the settlement who had been attracted by the sound of the gunfire.

"FOLKS," London said to the gathering crowd, "I'd like to show you a little something about shooting a Winchester rifle but I need a young man to volunteer to give me a hand."

Sean McNamara's son, a boy of about twelve pushed his way out of the crowd hollering, "Me ... Me ... let me help."

"Step right up here, young man," London said and started showing the people a skill they never knew existed."

Picking up the Winchester, London handed the boy a fist sized rock and told him to throw it up in the air. As the rock flew towards the edge of the Escarpment London pulled the Winchester to his shoulder and blasted the rock out of the air. Next London gave the boy progressively smaller targets until the last one thrown was no bigger than a child's fingernail. The pebble, clearly visible against the high, blue sky disappeared with London's final shot.

By this time Roll and Helen had joined the spectators and they applauded the performance with all the vigor of the rest of the settlers.

"Thank you all," London said, "but I think that's enough noise for one day. Now I think I'll go get some breakfast," and he started picking up his spent shell casings and cleaning up the scattered equipment.

London was at the kitchen table cleaning his guns when Colleen came in and started fixing eggs and coffee. "That was quite a show you put on out there," she said. "All the people loved it."

"That may be the only talent I have," London said modestly.

"No, that's not so," Colleen answered. "I finished reading the story of the Escarpment that you wrote and gave it to Father. It's very good."

"What did you think of Roll's talk last night?" London said abruptly changing the subject.

"What do you mean?" Colleen asked.

"Have you ever heard your father speak so openly about all of his private affairs before?" London said. "I felt like that talk was directed straight at me."

"How so?" Colleen asked.

London spent the next hour discussing in depth his thoughts about what he believed was the real meaning behind what Roll had said.

"So you believe that what Father said yesterday was putting down the ground work for what he wants to talk to you about today," Colleen said.

"Yes I do," London answered.

"If we carry this a step further," Colleen said, "could it be that what you did this morning could be the same kind of ground work for what your answer is going to be?"

London could see the concern in Colleen's face as she asked this question and suddenly he understood her concern.

"I hadn't thought of it that way, but I see what you're saying," he answered. "Just let me say I would never use violence against a friend and, when I came here, I considered Roll to be the best friend I had in the world."

"But you say that you want for us to leave here before winter," Colleen said. "Suppose he says no to that?"

"It is something we will have to work out," London answered. "Now I think I should go and talk with your parents and see what they have in mind. Want to come along?"

"You couldn't keep me away if there was a grizzly bear at that meeting," she said.

"You certainly could have phrased that differently," London said with a mock scowl. "Bears are not my favorite subject."

Roll and Helen were lounging around the house still resting up from the trip when Colleen and London came in the front door.

"Boy," Helen said, "that was some show you put on this morning. Roll had told me you were good but I never would have believed such shooting was possible if I hadn't seen it for myself."

"It was just something I thought the people here might get a kick out of," London said.

"They surely did," Roll said, "in fact, we all did."

"Coffee all around?" Helen said as she headed for the kitchen, a chorus of 'yeahs' following behind her.

"Let's sit in the office at the big table," Roll said and he led the way through the house. Almost before they had a chance to sit down, Helen joined them with a big tray containing a coffeepot, cups and fresh rolls with jam.

London waited until they were all comfortable and settled with their coffee before he said to Roll, "You mentioned last evening you wanted to talk to me. Is now a good time or did you want to do it privately?"

"This is fine," Roll answered. "It concerns everyone here at the table. What I want to talk about is the possibility of you wanting to leave the settlement. Helen and I have discussed this a lot and have come up with an offer that should interest you."

London said nothing and drank his coffee as he waited for Roll to continue.

"Here's the deal," Roll said. "First, Colleen stays until we get a new doctor trained. London can go to Denver and take over the running of our hotel. It has an attached saloon and gambling hall so he would get a chance to try his hand at something he wants to do without any financial risk. He would agree to return to the valley for six months every year. The house that was built for London would belong to the two of you after you're married. As soon as a new doctor is ..."

"Hold it a minute," London said impatiently. "Who do you have in mind to replace Colleen as a doctor?"

"Zack would have been my first choice," Roll said, "but now we'll have to go with Rebecca, Colleen's next oldest sister."

"Rebecca's only 16 years old," Colleen said. "If everything went perfect you're talking ten years before she would even be close to finishing her studies."

"I've considered that," Roll answered back somewhat abruptly.

Colleen looked at London and saw disbelief on his face. She looked at her mother but Helen looked down at the floor and wouldn't meet her eyes.

"What is this?" she said. "I can't really believe these suggestions you're making. Father, you've just said that you'll be taking over London's life and mine for the next ten years. Do you really expect us to go along with this?!"

"You hold it a minute, young lady," Roll said. "This is the deal your mother and I agreed to offer. These are not as you say—suggestions—but the arrangements you will either accept or reject as you see fit. Now if you'll let me go on explaining ..."

"Wait a second, Roll," London said. "You're getting way out of line here. I understand you have pretty much had your own way here in the valley and rightly so. You and Helen have made this paradise with your own hands but in spite of the fact that you two have become the King and Queen of the northwest, you are not my monarch."

"Now you listen for a second," Roll said as the voices got slightly louder. "These rules were in place before you ever came here and your arrival is not going to make me change them."

"I understand your rules and the reasons for them," London said, "but I feel that Colleen and I are exceptions. We want to get married and live our own life and no one is going to deny us our future."

Roll's face was turning red and he was rubbing the back of his neck with one hand as he started to get to his feet. London recognized the sign and leaned back in his chair and said, "Wait a minute, stay here. We've still got a lot to work out. If you get mad and walk out now, things are only going to get worse. Let's keep talking for a while yet."

Roll looked at London and then the two women at the table. He saw no real anger in London's face and recognized the pleading in the women's eyes, women he truly loved and he sat wearily back into his chair.

"How about this?" Roll said. "I understand some of this has been a shock to you two," he said indicating London and Colleen. "Maybe if we take a few days to think things over then we can talk more and try and work things out. I really don't want a family fuss here."

Some of the tension went out of the room and Helen finally looked up from her study of the floor and smiled at Colleen and London. "Yes, that probably would be best."

London sat on the ground near the edge of the Escarpment and watched the sun set. He had been sitting alone here for the last hour thinking about what had been said by Roll Jacobs. London didn't really believe that Roll was going to change the position he had taken in regards to the marriage of Colleen and their leaving the Escarpment.

After the heated discussion of that morning London felt that when Roll was faced with the ultimatum of leaving anything could happen.

Far off, the volcano was showing a slender stream of smoke that had a red tinge that might have been caused by the setting sun. London hoped so. He had come to believe in some of the superstitions that Chief Ouseph believed in so devoutly. The bears on the way to town closely followed by the Cheyenne attack. The volcano activity followed by the scarlet fever in the Indian camp. The second encounter with bears followed by this confrontation between he and Colleen and her parents.

As if to accent his feelings, far in the distance a ball of fire exploded from the mountain and shot high into the air. Within a few seconds he felt the ground shudder slightly and he looked back towards the settlement to watch as people came from their homes to stare into the distance at the offending volcano.

London turned and walked away from the edge of the Escarpment. He felt extreme apprehension about the future.

Chapter 18

London's coffee was cold and with a flip of the wrist he tossed it over the edge of the Escarpment. Like Diego Vargas, it would fall more than a mile before striking bottom.

With the prevailing attitudes it would be difficult to discuss plans for a wedding. Colleen had said she would like to have a minister come to the settlement to perform the ceremony. That suited him fine but what would Roll's reaction be? He seemed to be against everything at this point.

"You're up early," a voice said from behind him.

London turned to see Helen walking towards him along the fence. She had obviously crossed at a stile about a hundred yards away and he had not heard her coming.

"I didn't sleep very well," he said. "I've been sitting here thinking and watching the smoke from the volcano."

"It does seem to be getting thicker and darker," Helen said. "And I believe we all had trouble resting last night."

"Has anymore been said?" he asked.

"I haven't talked with Colleen," Helen said. "When I got up she was gone. When she has a problem she often goes riding alone. She says it helps her to think."

"How about Roll?" London said.

"He was in his library when I went to bed. I think he was finishing your story on the settlement. He sat there all night as far as I know," Helen said. "This is the first time he has ever had this type of disagreement to deal with."

"What do you think is going to happen?" London asked.

"I wish I knew," Helen replied. "We both approve of you and the marriage and are looking forward to it but Roll is just so upset about your wanting to leave. I certainly hope we can work it out. Like all mothers I'm excited about my daughter's wedding and the subsequent grandchildren."

"I don't know what I can say to ease your mind," London said.

"Yeah," Helen replied, "right now it's kind of a mess."

"When I first came out this morning I was thinking about how the Indians consider grizzly bears and the volcano to be bad luck," London said looking towards the north at the growing black cloud. "It looks like they could be in cahoots again."

"Roll laughs at me," Helen said, "but I've always been afraid of that damn mountain. He tells me I'm as superstitious as an Indian."

London tried to lighten the tone by saying, "Well, if Ouseph was here, knew about the bears and saw the mountain acting up, he would certainly have a lot to say about the subject."

"You're right," Helen said. "I should learn to accept nature for what it is, definite and unchangeable."

The sun was well up and London could feel the warmth through his flannel shirt. "I better get back to work," he said. "I'm working on building a small windmill to stir the mash in the brewery. If it works we won't have to maintain another power outlet."

"Do you need any help?" Helen asked.

"Not really," he said. "Sean McNamara has a special interest in the operation and he and I have just about got it finished."

"I'll walk back with you," Helen said. "Standing here and looking at the volcano certainly doesn't help me relax."

As they climbed the fence they saw Roll ride away from the corral and start up the valley at a canter.

"There goes another person who likes to be alone to think," Helen said.

It was late afternoon and the breeze from the south turned the windmill built over London's brewing shed. Inside the paddles in the large wooden vat moved slowly in a circle stirring the contents. The odor was foul and only a true beer lover would subject his sense of smell to such a nauseating mixture.

Sean and London were preparing to quit for the day and stood looking at their handiwork when Colleen came through the door and said, "I don't know how you can stand to work in here. I know your beer tastes good but this smell is unbearable."

"Come outside and let me show you what we've done," London said escorting her out the door. "We built the small windmill so we could do away with the steam pressure we were using to turn the paddles in the vat. Now the wind does the work and we can use the steam pressure for more important projects. All we have to do now is check it every couple of hours and wait for it to be ready to put into kegs."

"Well, I guess you could call this progress," she said.

"I'd certainly like to think so," Sean chimed in.

"So what brings you out to this smelly place?" London asked.

"I came to get you for dinner," she said taking his arm and leading him away from his partner.

London waved his hand in Sean's direction and followed Colleen towards her house. "Father has gone to see Ouseph," Colleen said, "and Mother thought you might like to join us. Since Father will be gone there shouldn't be as much tension."

"Yeah," London answered, "I talked to your mother for a good while this morning and she doesn't know what to do any more than we do."

"I was in the trees resting when I saw father ride up the valley this morning but he didn't see me," Colleen said. "He had full saddle bags, shelter half and a bedroll tied to the back of his saddle. I knew what he was doing. He likes to go off by himself when he has some thinking to do. I'm like him in that respect."

"What did you decide today?" London asked.

"Not a thing! ... not a damned thing!" Colleen said and London laughed at her mild profanity.

"Then let's go eat and we'll worry about this later," he said.

After dinner London sat on a chair near the sink as the women washed and dried the dishes. Helen was busy explaining a drawing she had shown them during the meal. It was a gas stove with burners on top that had flames that could be adjusted up and down like a light on the wall.

"It doesn't exactly suit me," Helen said, "but it's a start. I think when Roll looks at the drawing he'll have suggestions that will make it better."

London tried to concentrate on what she was saying but his mind kept wandering. After the violent reaction of the previous evening he was uncomfortable sitting in the kitchen of Roll's home. During the meal the women had prattled away and his only requirement had been to nod and agree whenever he was included in the conversation.

What concerned London the most was what to expect the next time that he and Roll came face to face. Suppose he forbids the marriage unless all of his conditions were met. Or worse, forbid the marriage altogether. What if the confrontation became physical—even violent? He wasn't afraid of Roll but that would not be the way to start a marriage. There was only one thing he could do!

London stood up so quickly he startled the women as he said, "Ladies, there is only one solution to this problem. It's up to me to work it out with Roll. One way or another I'll make peace with him and patch this thing up. I'll be talking to him as soon as he gets back. Now I'm gonna' walk up to the barn and be alone for a while."

Outside, London found Henri Merroux headed for the corral and he fell into step with the Frenchman.

"You going up to take a look at the bear skins?" Henri asked. "They're hanging in the barn."

"Not really," London answered. "If I never see another grizzly it'll be too soon."

"Yeah, that was kind of close," Henri said, "but at least we're going to have enough dog food to last for a long time. We butchered the carcasses and hung them in the ice house and there's more than a ton of meat and the skins are going to make fine rugs."

"Not in my house," London replied. "I don't need any reminder of those bears."

"Don't feel bad about getting thrown," Henri said. "Not many can ride those big Percherons with a saddle or bridle."

"Never-the-less I still feel a little foolish," London answered.

They reached the corral and London picked up a rope halter and walked into the herd singling out his horse. He slipped the halter over its head and led it into a stall where he began brushing and combing the animal. He dumped an extra measure of oats into the feed box and patted the horse's neck while it ate.

Henri had finished his inspection of the barn and the herd and now stood outside the stall watching London.

"There's talk that you and Colleen might be getting hitched," Henri said. "Any truth to the rumor?"

"There's been some talk between her and me about such a thing," London answered, "but nothing is real definite at the moment." London laughed to himself as he said this last and thought, what an understatement.

"If it means anything, all the talk I've heard is favorable to a wedding," Henri said. "When you first came here everybody took their time making up their minds about you. As you know we don't get many newcomers here so your showing up was a real event in our lives."

"I appreciate your kind words," London said.

"I'm going back now," Henri said, "you coming?"

"No, not yet," London said, "you go ahead."

After a few more minutes with his horse, London walked out of the stall and sat down on the edge of a manger, his mind spinning like a dust devil. If everyone's having this much trouble deciding what to do, we all must be a miserable bunch he was thinking.

"Howdy cowboy, you lonesome?" a voice said from behind him.

For the second time that day London had been startled by a woman's voice. "I didn't hear you walk up," he said to Colleen who was standing in the doorway.

"I know you said you wanted to be alone but my curiosity got the best of me," she said. "Do you really think you'll be able to work things out with father?"

"Yes I do," London said positively.

"You sound pretty sure of yourself," she replied. "Do you know what you're going to say?"

"Not exactly," London answered, "but your father is an intelligent man and I'm sure I'll be able to get him to understand our point of view."

"Okay cowboy, I believe you," Colleen said. Now, just to change the subject, have you ever seen what's up in the hay mow of this barn?"

"No I haven't," he replied. "Why?"

"Come with me, cowboy," Colleen said as she started to climb the ladder. "There's something up there I want you to take a look at."

Now they were slowly walking back towards the houses, hand in hand. "Yes," she said, "I suppose the volcano is beautiful at night but it still makes me uneasy. The power is what bothers me the most. Who knows what that mountain is capable of doing."

Almost in answer to her question the volcano shot a stream of fire into the air and they could feel a slight tremble in the ground.

"I guess you shouldn't say bad things about Mount Saint Helen," he said. "Seems like she objects."

"At least it was only a mild objection," Colleen answered as she moved closer to London putting her arm around his waist.

"As long as I get that reaction, I don't mind," he said as he turned and pulled her close, kissing her soft, full mouth.

Colleen leaned back and said, "By the way, I came up here to ask you something else. I've got guard duty up the valley tomorrow morning at ten o'clock. You wanna' come along?"

"Just the two of us up there all alone for twenty four hours? I'd love to go," and he kissed her once again.

Chapter 19

When London awoke the sky looked strange from his upstairs bedroom window until he looked and saw that the wind was blowing the smoke from the volcano directly over the settlement. It was hard to make out the sunrise back to the east. A bad sign the Indians would say on a day when he might be meeting with Roll and needing all the good luck he could get.

He made coffee and ate his bacon and eggs along with some fresh bread he found on his kitchen table when he got home last night.

Carrying a cup of coffee he strolled to the brewery shed and found the windmill was doing its job. He walked back home and began cleaning his Winchester as he finished off his coffee. That done he went onto the front porch and watched the smoke from the volcano until he saw Colleen approaching. She was carrying a pair of saddlebags and a white flour sack that looked to be half full.

She set her parcels on his porch and explained in one word. "Picnic," she said. "Enough for three meals."

"I'll go get the horses," he said. "You wanta' come along?"

"Sure," she answered and they started walking towards the barn.

After saddling the horses and picking up the packages from London's porch they began their ride to the entrance of the settlement. The day was clear except for the smoke from the volcano and they cantered their mounts up the center of the valley. London had slid his Winchester in a saddle scabbard and Colleen had one of the Henry rifles in her rig.

"How come you don't have one of the new Winchesters?" London asked.

"I've had this rifle for a while and I know how it shoots," she said. "I've never had a chance to shoot one of the new rifles so before I take one out I'd like to practice with it a little bit."

"Maybe you should have brought one along with some extra shells and we could have done some shooting," he said.

Colleen shook her head and said, "If we did any shooting up here at the lookout station we'd have everyone in the settlement headed our way."

"Oh yeah, I never thought of that," London replied. "Who are we relieving up here?"

"Peter Digondo's oldest boy. He's seventeen now and started doing guard duty just this year. He likes it and whenever he's up here he carves things out of wood, animals and toys and such. He's very talented and I'm sure he'll have something to show us when we get there."

"We'll know soon enough," London said, "because that looks like him at the tree line."

Colleen looked ahead, squinting, and soon made out what London had seen earlier, a rider sitting an Appaloosa just back in the trees. She raised her arm in greeting and the boy came riding towards them.

"Hi Colleen. Mornin' Mister London," he called out. "They send two people up here today? What's goin' on?"

"London just came along to keep me from getting lonesome," Colleen said with a wink.

"Aw heck, I understand," the boy said blushing and looking down at his saddle.

"Did you carve anything while you were up here, Andre?" Colleen asked.

"Yeah I did. Look at this," the boy said.

On a flat piece of wood the boy had carved a picture in three-dimensional relief of the view looking north from the Escarpment with the volcano right in the middle. He had used a piece of charcoal to darken the white wood in places to make shadows and it was a positive work of the finest art.

"I made this for you," he said with a shy smile as he handed it to Colleen.

"This is really beautiful, Andre. Thank you very much," she said.

"Now I gotta' go," he said. "I promised Constance Merroux I'd help her break a new colt this afternoon. I'll see you both later," and he headed down the valley.

The small spring at the edge of the trees had clean, fresh water and had been the favorite resting spot for guard duty. The brush and trees had been carefully groomed so as to permit a full view of the valley. Colleen had spread a blanket on the ground and they had eaten their lunch of fried chicken and baked beans as they waited for the bottles of beer to cool in the nearby water. A jug of wine also cooled beside the beer for their evening meal.

Next to the spring was a towering oak tree with a ladder nailed to one side that led to a board platform about thirty feet up. It was a good observation point and a place to go if a bear became bothersome. The horses were left saddled and tied lightly nearby in case they were needed quickly.

Colleen and London sat in the shade, their backs against a tree and their shoulders touching. The third big rumble of the afternoon shook the ground and made the water in the spring ripple. From where they were sitting the trees blocked their view of the volcano but the smoke was still thick overhead.

"Has it ever gone on this long before?" London asked

"Not with the ground tremors," Colleen answered. "Sometimes before we have had this much smoke but never the two together."

"Well, it probably won't last much longer and besides after dark it won't matter anyway," London said. He was referring to the rules for the guard. As long as there was daylight you watched the valley but once it got dark you could rest.

The nighttime shelter was a tent back about fifty feet and it was well hidden and a haven from insects. It could keep a person dry in the rain and the buffalo robes inside made a comfortable and warm place to sleep in any weather.

London had just walked to the spring for a couple bottles of beer when a rider came into view entering the valley. They both swung into their saddles and moved to the edge of the trees where they could see without being seen.

Before Colleen could even raise the binoculars to her eyes London said, "It's Roll. He's headed this way," and they rode out to meet him.

Roll looked from one to the other and said, "Howdy, is everything okay?"

"Sure," Colleen said back. "You're the only person we've seen since we got here. How about you?"

"I'm fine," Roll answered. "I just went off to spend some time thinking about things but all I got done was feeling the ground shake."

"It has been shaking pretty steady and there's been a lot of smoke and fire," Colleen said.

"Any new cracks in the ground?" Roll asked.

"No. Not that we saw," London answered.

"Then I better be getting back to the settlement," Roll said and turned his horse to head down the valley.

"Wait a minute," London said. "I want to ride along with you for a ways. There is something we need to talk about, just you and me."

"I agree," Roll replied. "Let's ride a ways."

Colleen flashed London a pleading expression as he said to her, "I'll be back in a little bit," and followed after Roll.

The two men walked their horses for several minutes in silence, each waiting for the other to open the conversation. Finally Roll said, "You wanted to talk, go ahead."

"Okay," London said. "Roll, you've put Colleen and me into a nearly impossible position. She loves you and all of her family and doesn't want to do anything that would make any of you unhappy. I feel much the same way. I consider you to be the only real friend I have in the world. Colleen and I would do almost anything to keep peace here in the valley."

"That's nice," Roll said. "Now tell me the 'but'."

"All right," London answered. "But we won't live our lives by your rules. If our future is somewhere beyond this valley you'll just have to accept that."

Roll didn't look at London as he started to talk. "While I've been alone the last day or so I've thought about nothing else than what you just said. I told you the other night what the deal was for you and Colleen. Now I've decided to make it a slightly better offer. If you want to go to Denver and run the hotel there, Helen and I will deed it over to you and Colleen as a wedding present. You can go there and run the operation for up to six months a year. The other six months you will spend here at the settlement. Of course Colleen will stay here while you're gone, at least until we get another person trained as a doctor."

"Well, at least we're talking," London said trying to lighten the mood.

Roll would have none of it. He kept his horse walking at a steady pace as he looked at London and said, "This is the only deal there is going to be. You can take it or leave it. I've made as many concessions as I'm going to make. I'm not going to change the rules of the settlement just for you!"

"I don't see it where you've changed much of anything. You invited me here as a guest and now you want to make me a prisoner," London said. "What if I don't go along with your deal?"

"You misunderstand," Roll answered back sharply. "That's the only way it can be if there's going to be a marriage."

"Roll, you're way out of line!" London said. "You are not going to tell Colleen and I how we are going to live our lives."

"I'm telling her she can't go with you unless these conditions are met!" Roll almost shouted.

"How could you do this to your own daughter?" London demanded. "She should never have to make such a decision."

"Your decision is what set the wheels in motion," Roll said. "I built this place and have lived by these rules for more than twenty years. I won't give it all up now."

London sagged in his saddle, sure that further talk was useless and said the words he hoped he wouldn't need to say. "What if we decide to leave in spite of your objections?"

"I'd stop you," Roll said quietly.

"How would you do that?" London asked looking Roll straight in the eyes.

Roll stared back and said, "With any means necessary."

The horses had stopped and the two men had reached an impasse. London spoke next saying, "I'm not Diego Vargas."

"Well, it's going to be your call to make," Roll said as he kicked his horse into motion and left London alone in the middle of the valley.

London stepped down from his horse and stood looking after Roll. After a couple of minutes he started leading his mount back to where Colleen waited. He was in no hurry to get there.

Boy, oh boy, did I make a mess of that, he thought. Was it me, him or both of us that were being unreasonable? Damned if I know. Now I'm going to have to tell Colleen something about what had been said.

The ground shook under his feet in still another tremor and London turned and looked back towards the volcano and said out loud, "You really are bad luck, you son-of-a-bitch. Now look at the mess I'm into."

London looked up at the red orb of the sun barely visible through the smoke that filled the sky and estimated a little over two hours before dark. He swung into the saddle and headed for Colleen to give her the bad news.

Roll pushed his horse slightly as he headed for home. He was not looking forward to filling Helen in on the conversation he had had with London.

"So what are we going to do?" Colleen asked London when he finished telling her what Roll had said. "Do you think there is any chance that father might give in just a little bit?"

London put his arm around her waist and was heading back for their seats under the tree when another tremor ran through the ground. "Right now I'd say that Roll is as unstable as the volcano. It doesn't look very good to me."

Helen looked across the kitchen table at Roll and asked, "What do you think is going to happen? Will they understand your ... our position and at least try to cooperate?"

"I don't know," Roll said. "The only other alternative I have left is to give up the integrity of the settlement and go along with everything they want. I hate to even consider surrendering our paradise."

London took Colleen's hand as he asked another question. "Do you think Helen will try and get Roll to relax a little bit? Maybe she can see how out of hand the situation has become. Could she and would she try to influence Roll in our behalf."

"I don't know," Colleen answered. "She has always stood solidly behind anything father did or wanted to do."

"What do you think Colleen is going to do?" Roll asked Helen. "I'm sure she and London have discussed this at length. Will she be willing to stay here until we can get another doctor trained?"

"She's your daughter too," Helen said. "She will probably do just as you have taught her all of her life and go her own way and do what she thinks is right. Whatever she does, it will be a hard decision for her."

"You and Father wouldn't fight, would you?" Colleen asked.

"No," London said emphatically, "I'd never let that happen. I think that your father believes he is losing his daughter, his paradise

176

and the rules he has lived by for nearly half his life all at one time. He remembers what he did with Diego Vargas and I think that also preys on his mind."

Another tremor caused the surface of the water in the spring to ripple.

Roll watched his coffee slosh around in the cup as another tremor caused the kitchen table to shake. The fire, smoke and movement were making Helen a nervous wreck. She got up from the table and walked to the window where she could look towards the Escarpment.

"This is the worst ever," Helen said. "We're going to be very lucky if we don't end up with another fissure in the ground."

"That damned volcano is the least of our worries right now," Roll said. "What we got to figure out is … Ouch!—dammit—what's this?"

A cup and saucer had slid from the top of the highboy behind Roll and hit him in the back of the head.

Helen turned from the window and looked back across the room just in time to see the cupboard start to tip forward, spilling it's contents onto the floor with a crash. Now a rumbling noise seemed to fill the room and when she looked back towards the Escarpment her view had changed. No longer was she looking straight out into space, now she was looking more down into the valley beyond the rim.

Everything in the kitchen was sliding towards Helen. Roll, slipping and sliding, managed to jump across the table and pull her out through the front door before she was squashed against the wall.

London and Colleen had jumped to their feet at the last violent shake and now they found themselves bouncing and rolling as the ground started to undulate. Colleen lost the skin from her hands and tore the knees out of her jeans while London sliced his forearm open on a sharp rock. Colleen was stunned but London recovered quickly enough to make a grab for the horses and managed to catch both pair of reins.

Helen and Roll careened across the yard as they fell downhill towards the edge of the Escarpment. The fall became steeper until everything behind them was following in their path as the earth continued to fall away and the entire settlement shot out into space. A million fingernails on a blackboard could not have caused that kind of screaming. The dust and rumbling only added to the chaos.

Colleen clawed her way to where London was holding the horses but the animals, crazy with fear, were almost impossible to control. It was all London could do just keeping hold of the reins.

The houses were torn to pieces and they went over the edge in a mass of debris mixed with rock, earth and people. Roll and Helen were still holding on to each other as they went flying into space with no chance of survival. The rumbling crash mingled with the screams clear to the base of the Escarpment thousands of feet below.

Once they were mounted, London and Colleen pushed their horses hard for the settlement. As they came down the center of the valley in the twilight they could see a huge cloud of dust rising up in the distance near the Escarpment. Far ahead on the right where the power station and the sawmill would be located they could see a huge fire soaring into the darkening sky.

Out of the gloom Colleen and London saw a rider coming towards them. It was Constance Merroux and she was riding hard.

"HEY ... HEY ... HEY!" London yelled, "SLOW DOWN!"

Constance pulled her horse to a skidding halt as she yelled,

"They're all gone. Everybody is gone. The houses, the people, everything went over the edge. We saw it all."

London slid to the ground and grabbed the halter of Constance's horse. "Get down and tell me what happened," he said.

Constance dismounted as did Colleen and the two women put their arms around each other, the older comforting the younger. Constance's face was covered with dust and her cheeks streaked with tracks of tears that were still coursing down from her eyes to her chin.

"We were up at the corral," Constance managed to gasp and we heard this noise. "At first we thought it was just another earth tremor but then we saw the settlement start to tip and slide. Before we knew what was happening, the edge of the Escarpment where the houses were went over the edge. Everything just disappeared," and she started to sob hysterically.

Colleen held the girl at arms' length by the shoulders and stared, unable to speak. "What? Who? What?" she stammered.

London made a little more sense as he asked, "You mean the houses and the people all went over the edge? They're all gone?"

"As far as I know," Constance answered. "Andre was getting a lantern from the barn and going to where the houses had disappeared when I left him. He told me come get you two."

"We better get on down there," London said as he helped Constance back on her horse.

Thirty minutes later the three could see a lantern moving up ahead and they slowed down as they got close. Beyond the lantern where the lights from the houses should have been it was pitch black and a tremendous cloud of dust rolled up over the edge of the Escarpment.

As they neared the lantern, Andre's voice came out of the dark and said, "You better stop there. From here on there's nothing but a big hole where the houses used to be and the hole goes down further than I can see."

London stopped his horse and told the two women to wait while he went forward to see what Andre was talking about. Suddenly he reached the edge of the Escarpment nearly half a mile back from where it should have been.

"Can you see anything?" London asked Andre.

"Not a thing," the boy replied. "Before it was completely dark, looking down from here was just like looking over the edge before the landslide. As near as I can tell it goes straight down from here."

"Have you heard anything like maybe somebody yelling?" London asked.

"Not a sound except sometimes more rocks or dirt falling," Andre said.

"Let's get back from the edge and decide what we're going to do," London said as he headed back to where the two women waited.

"Tell me!" Colleen demanded as he approached her.

"I can't tell for sure but it looks like a landslide took the whole set-tlement over the cliff. It's so dark you can't see much and the dust near the edge is as thick as fog," London said.

"But what about the people?" Colleen asked. "Where are mother and father and the little ones ... the rest of the people? Where are they?"

Neither London nor Andre said anything.

"THEY CAN'T BE," Colleen screamed. "Not that quick. Not EVERYONE," and she collapsed on the ground sobbing as London knelt down and tried to comfort her.

Several minutes went by before Colleen and the rest partially recovered their composure and Colleen asked, "What are we going to do now?"

"I'd like to go over the edge and have a look," London said, "but not in the dark. We should go to the barn and bring all the rope we can find and be ready to start at first light."

"There is a trail that you can take to get down to the bottom," Colleen said, "but it is dangerous. Maybe the landslide has made it impassable but, like you said, we won't know until daylight."

"Okay," London said. "Colleen and I will make the climb at first light. Andre, you and Constance will stay here in case we don't get back. If we don't, you'll have to tell Ouseph what happened and go to

180

Denver and notify Roll's family and the rest. See the president of the bank in Denver and he'll know what to do."

"Colleen," London went on, "you and Constance stay here and Andre and I will go to the barn and gather up all the rope we can find. Stay back from the edge and we'll be back before you know it."

Andre brought in a team of Percherons and put their working harnesses on them while London gathered up all the rope he could find and together they loaded it onto the horses along with three more lanterns and a can of coal oil. After filling several canteens they headed back to where the women waited.

In the morning light they could see that the volcano had ceased to smoke and belch fire and there had been no more tremors. Colleen led the way to where a trail had led to the bottom of the Escarpment. Whether it was still passable remained to be seen. Using the team of horses as an anchor they started feeding rope over the edge and then London started down. The plan was to wait until he found a second anchor. Then more rope could be lowered down to bridge any parts of the path that were unstable.

In some places the trail was clear for travel but as London passed the halfway point, dirt and debris caused more and more trouble. He fastened ropes along the path so it would be possible to climb back out after they had finished exploring the bottom of the landslide.

So far London had not seen or heard anything at the base of the Escarpment.

Colleen joined him as the rocks from the landslide came into sight. It was now nearly noon and the sun had reached down to where they labored so they rested for a few minutes and drank some water before Colleen urged London on, hoping against hope they would find some survivors.

Down at the bottom, the pile of rubble that had fallen from the top was enormous. It was more than three hundred feet high and spread over several acres of ground.

Colleen and London started their search but all they found were huge plates of limestone and rocks. It appeared that the ground on which the settlement had set turned over in the air and buried everything and everyone under thousands of tons of earth.

Colleen sat down on a flat rock, her elbows on her knees and her face in her hands. London stood at her side trying in some way to ease her pain. They were both covered with sweaty dust and their clothing was torn in a dozen places from the climb down.

Colleen's eyes were dry but were just hollows in her face as she looked up at London and said, "Nothing. Not a stick of wood, not a piece of paper, absolutely everything is gone. How can that be?" and a racking sob shook her body.

London felt her pain and wished there were something he could say, but there was nothing that would ease her pain.

After a few minutes London said, "We're going to have to start back up. With the ropes in place we won't have much trouble unless it gets dark on us."

"I suppose," she said as she got to her feet and began, zombie-like, to climb the face of the Escarpment.

The four survivors sat in the barn drinking hot tea and nibbling on deer meat cooked over an open fire. They had found a few supplies that had escaped the fire at the woodworking shop.

Now London was talking. "We'll take a six-horse hitch of Percherons with one of the big wagons and tie six Appaloosas on behind. When we get to a spot close to the Indian camp we can leave everything with Andre and Constance while we ride to see Ouseph and tell him what has happened. How does that sound so far?"

"What about the other animals, cows, pigs, chickens, and the rest?" Constance asked.

"All we can do is open all the gates and turn them loose here in the valley," Colleen said. "They should be safe until Ouseph can send some men to collect them."

"After we talk to the Indians," London said, "we'll need to stop in town and tell the storekeeper so he can adjust his orders. We can check with Ouseph and find out if he has anything at the store and arrange for Red Fox or someone to pick it up."

"What about the kids in the Indian camp?" Andre asked.

"Oh-oh, I hadn't thought of them," Colleen said.

London thought for a minute and said, "Maybe we better wait until we get to Ouseph's camp before we decide."

"What do you think we ought to do with these two?" Colleen asked indicating Andre and Constance.

"Right now I guess we'll have to keep them with us and take them on to Denver," London said. "We have a lot of telegrams to send and business to transact. I guess they'll just have to come along."

"Really? Denver?" Andre said. In spite of the disaster the adults could see a slight crack in the teenagers' depression.

"I've never been further than the store or the Indian camp," Constance said.

"Me neither," Andre echoed.

"But where will we live in Denver?" Constance asked with some apprehension.

"Don't you worry," Colleen said. "We'll find a place and you two can stay with London and me."

"Are you guys gonna' get married then?" Andre asked excitedly.

"Just as soon as we get to Denver," London said pulling Colleen close against his side.

That night they all wrapped up in blankets and slept in the hay. Once during the night Colleen woke up screaming and only after London held and comforted her for a long time did she finally get some rest.

The next morning at first light they were up and preparing the wagon. An hour later they were headed out of the valley.

They never made it to the Indian camp. London was hitching up the horses for the second day on the trail when Chief Ouseph and a large group of his people came riding into view. He had thought when

183

the terrible tremors had shaken their camp that the settlement, being so much closer to the mountain, could be in serious trouble and they immediately had set out to bring aid to their neighbors.

London walked towards the Indian troop and greeted Ouseph and the others as they slid from their horses.

"London my friend," Ouseph asked, "what has happened? Why are just you four here?"

"As you foretold," London said, "the Rumbling Hills have brought disaster. We are all that are left alive from the settlement."

All from the Indian camp had crowded around to hear what London was saying and there was a collective intake of breaths followed by disbelieving silence. Morning ran to Colleen and took her in her arms.

"Please, tell us all," Red Fox said.

"Let's do it this way," London suggested. "Andre saw the landslide that took the settlement over the edge of the Escarpment. After he tells you everything he saw, Colleen and I will fill you in on what we did."

As the people gathered to hear the stories, London stirred up the fire and added a few sticks and branches. so coffee and tea could be prepared. While he was working London noticed the Winchester that Red Fox was carrying and made a mental note to ask Ouseph for a couple of extra rifles and ammunition to give them more fire power on their trip to Denver.

After all of the story telling was over, Ouseph sought out London and Colleen for a private talk. "This will be a time of adjustment for all of us," he said, "not just because of the loss of our friends and relatives but because it will require so many changes in what has become our lifestyle."

London spoke quickly saying, "Chief, Colleen and I will be married as soon as possible after reaching Denver. We will continue to assist you with supplies and in all other ways as Roll has done in the past."

"My friend London," Ouseph said, "my people have come to

think of you as a true ally. Your marriage to Colleen would bind us even closer. If we can continue many of the traditions started by Roll Jacobs, it would honor the Chopunnish as well as his memory."

"Then I say this," London said somewhat formally. "Before winter comes, Colleen and I will arrange to have a house built at the entrance to the valley where the guard was always posted. We will spend time here each year and work towards rebuilding in the valley."

"It would be good to keep the plans alive," Ouseph said. "Let us drink tea and talk of the future and allow the dead to be with the dead."

Colleen stood up straight and looked at Ouseph with great respect as she said, "Yes, let us do that," and she followed Ousepf towards the fire.

Chapter 20

London came out of the courthouse in Denver and climbed on the wagon seat next to Colleen. "Where's the nearest church?" he asked.

"Keep driving down this street," Colleen answered. "You can see the steeple just ahead on the right."

The minister was out front sweeping the sidewalk when the wagon stopped. He looked up to see no fewer than eight children peering out from under the canvas cover, six of them being younger children of about the same age and two being older teenagers. The man driving and the woman next to him were rough dressed and dirty from the trail. The minister was well acquainted with this type of people.

"Howdy folks," the minister said. "What can I do for you this fine morning?"

"We would like to get married," the attractive woman on the front seat said.

The minister surveyed the crew in the wagon and said, "Yes ma'am, I can see where you might. Do you have a license?"

"Sure do Reverend,' London said as he vaulted from the wagon seat and turned to help the woman down before handing the paper to the minister.

"Then come along with me and bring all your young'uns. Before you know it you will be Mister and Misses ... a ... let me see," and he studied the paper for a minute before he went on. "Ah yes, here it is ... Towne ... Mister and Misses ..."

His last words were drowned out by Colleen's yell. "WHAT!! ... your last name is TOWNE ... Oh no."

The inside of the church smelled of fresh paint, new lumber and varnish. The summer heat amplified the claustrophobic feeling for the children who accompanied London and Colleen through the large front door. The semi-finished pews looked as though they had been designed to torture the occupants rather than make worship more comfortable.

"Right this way," the minister said as he conducted the group down the center aisle and up to the pulpit.

Chattering away like the happy person he was, the preacher soon had everyone situated to his approval and the ceremony was over almost before the participants knew what was happening.

London barely had time to kiss the bride before the preacher was shaking his hand and welcoming him and his family to Denver.

"Reverend," London said, "these are not our children. We're the only survivors of the Roll Jacobs settlement north of here. There was an earthquake and these two teenagers and six children were the only others to survive."

"Are you saying that Roll Jacobs, the famous mountain man, is dead?" the preacher asked.

Colleen replied saying, "Yes, he was my father and they were all killed. My mother, my family, my friends, everyone was ..." She stood straight and took a deep breath, "killed. Now we have to get on with our lives."

"I'm so sorry for your pain," the minister replied. "Is there anything I can do to help, a place to stay, helping with the children, food, clothing ...?"

"No thank you," Colleen said. "We'll be able to get along just fine."

"Where will you be staying?" the minister asked.

London and Colleen started back down the aisle and as they emerged from the church Colleen pointed down the street towards the center of Denver and said, "We'll be staying at the new Towne House Hotel."

"Never heard of a hotel by that name," the minister said.

"Well you have now," Colleen said. "My husband just got it as a wedding present, new name and all. This is where we will be starting our new life and you can be sure that before long Denver will know that we're here to stay."

The End